SILENT NIGHT DREAMS

Mistletoe Meadows
Book 8

JESSIE GUSSMAN

Acknowledgments

Cover art by Covers and Cupcakes
Narration by Jay Dyess
Author Services by CE Author Assistant

Listen to the unabridged audio for FREE performed by Jay Dyess on the Say with Jay channel on YouTube. Get early access to all of Jay's recordings and listen to Jessie's books before they're available to the general public, plus get daily Bible readings by Jay and bonus scenes by becoming a Say with Jay channel member.

Books in the Mistletoe Meadows Sweet Christmas romance series:
1. Sleigh Bell Dreams
2. Icicle Dreams
3. Sugarplum Dreams
4. Christmas Dreams
5. Holly Jolly Dreams
6. Candy Cane Dreams
7. Mistletoe Dreams
8. Silent Night Dreams
9. Candlelight Dreams

Chapter One

"Ten minutes until showtime."

Grace Dempsey looked up at the stage assistant, the comb clutched so tightly it bit into her hand.

"Thank you so much," she said, inclining her head graciously, pleased to note her voice did not tremble.

"The crowd is sold out. There are people standing in the back! I've never seen it this packed!" The stage assistant's cheeks were flushed, and he clasped his hands together, giving her the kind of look that was usually reserved for mega rock stars or A-list movie stars.

Not a classically trained concert pianist like herself.

She waited until the door closed before she allowed the starch in her back to drain out, and she slumped down, deliberately setting the comb down on her dressing table.

You've got to get it together. Everyone is expecting to see a performance like last time. You can't let them down.

She had no sooner thought that than cramps squeezed her abdomen painfully, and she only hesitated a moment before she jumped up from her seat, running to the restroom.

She barely made it in time. But it didn't take long because she'd already emptied out everything in her digestive system from both ends. Her hands slid on the doorway as she leaned against it, her knees shaking, her forehead hot and clammy, hands cold and clammy.

How was she going to go out and perform? She couldn't even sit at her dressing table without having to run to the restroom.

And what was wrong with her? She'd never had this kind of problem before. She'd always been eager to perform, excited. She looked forward to it.

But today, today, she was scared to death to go out in front of that huge crowd.

Everyone was expecting her to be able to play like she had last time. And the time before that. And the time before that. And she could, she knew she could. She just had to play the way she always had.

Except that the idea of going out made her turn right back around and head back into the restroom.

She couldn't go out like this. There was just no way.

But she couldn't cancel. Not at this late moment.

Her phone buzzed, and she finished washing her hands, drying them on the towel and noticing that they shook so badly she could barely hang it back up.

On trembling legs, she walked back out into her dressing room and picked up her phone.

It was her manager.

Clearing her throat, she stared at her phone. Could she tell Sasha that she couldn't go out on stage? It would be unheard of for her to cancel at such late notice, unless there was a serious problem, probably requiring hospitalization. If she wasn't dead, she would perform. That's the way she'd been brought up, that was her mindset, except...

She took a deep breath. What was wrong with her?

Her hands trembled and she almost dropped her phone. How could she hit the notes with her fingers shaking so hard?

Finally, she swiped and put the phone to her ear.

"Hello?" she asked, in the cultured, casual tone that she always used. To her ears, it didn't sound like anything was wrong. How could she fake it so convincingly and yet be so utterly sure that she absolutely could not go out on stage?

"Grace. I just wanted to let you know that the president has made a last-minute decision to attend. He is settled in his seat, and he is looking forward to your performance. I just spoke with him, and he gushed over your last concert. He has several members of his cabinet with him, and they are eager to hear our American talent."

Grace swallowed hard, but she knew she wasn't going to be able to hold down the dry heaves for long.

"I can't." The words came out choked, as much as she would like to have continued to be able to speak in her unaffected tone.

"I'm sorry?" Sasha said, like the idea that Grace might have said that she couldn't do it was absolutely ludicrous.

"I'm sorry. I want to be able to, but I absolutely cannot." At least she had gotten better control of her vocal cords. Why couldn't she have been a singer?

But she still couldn't go out on that stage. The idea of performing in front of all of those people made her feel like her knees were going to collapse, and she felt hot and cold and absolutely petrified, like she needed to go hide somewhere. Without even thinking about it, her eyes darted about the room, looking under the chair, trying to figure out if she would fit there.

She was a grown woman. What was wrong with her?

"What?"

"I said I can't."

"I'm sorry, you can't what?" Sasha said, still obviously having trouble grasping the reality.

"I cannot go out on stage. You're going to have to cancel the concert."

Where would she go? What could she do? If she canceled this... She could still make next week's performance, except... The idea of performing anything made her feel like her throat was rotating like helicopter blades, and her stomach was attached for the ride. She needed to get out of here. She needed to escape.

"Are you sick? Should I call an ambulance?" Sasha asked, her concern reaching through the phone.

Sasha was not coldhearted, but she was not going to understand that Grace was pretty sure all this was, was a panic attack.

"Yes. An ambulance."

There, she'd admitted it. She felt a touch of relief, but mostly, admitting it had allowed it to have the upper hand, and she sank to the floor.

"I need an ambulance," she managed to grind out.

"All right. I'm hanging up right now and I'm calling an ambulance, and then I'll be right there. Five minutes tops. Hold on."

The phone went dead, and Grace allowed her head to rest on the cold floor. It didn't really make her feel better, but at least the heavy, suffocating weight of the thought of going out in front of all those people was no longer in the forefront of her mind, and she slowly felt like her insides were calming down. Her chest only ached a little, and she no longer felt like she needed to stay in the bathroom indefinitely.

What had happened? Was that what stage fright was? Could she go through with her performance anyway? If she tried to go out, would she have some kind of attack while she performed? Or should she just assume that once she started playing she would feel better.

The idea made her stomach clench again, and she shook her head quickly, although she was alone in the dressing room. Absolutely not. She couldn't start playing, not when there was a chance that she would end up with some kind of attack. Maybe she really was having a heart attack. She had heard that sometimes symptoms presented themselves differently in women than in men, and her chest really did hurt.

She only had a few more seconds to herself before the door burst in and Sasha hurried over, kneeling at her side.

"What's the matter?" Sasha asked, breathless.

"I think I might be dying. Heart attack? A stroke? I'm not sure, but I'm scared. And I feel terrible. Like Doomsday is here." That was a little dramatic, but it was the truth. She felt like she was going to die.

"Hold on. The ambulance is here now, and I have Penny bringing them back. They'll be here in a m—"

She didn't get to finish her sentence before the door burst open, without even a perfunctory knock. Grace couldn't remember the last time someone had come into her dressing room with such disrespect, except that she'd given into the fear, and she was overwhelmed by it. There had to be something seriously wrong, something life or death. It was a heart attack, or some kind of fast-growing cancer, or something. There had to be something wrong.

Chapter Two

"I'm sorry. There is absolutely nothing wrong. Your heart is healthier than mine, according to all of our tests. I'll discharge you with a note to go see your PCP. I recommend you talk to them about some anxiety medication."

"Anxiety?" Grace couldn't help it, her voice sounded weak and strained.

She glanced across the bed where Sasha stood, her arms folded over her chest, her brows drawn. Sasha could not possibly be happy to hear that there actually was nothing wrong with her, other than a little bit of anxiety.

It didn't seem like a little. It seemed like a lot. So much that she thought she had been going to die.

"Anxiety. What you most likely experienced was a panic attack. The symptoms are all there. Feeling like you're losing control of your bodily functions, absolute fear, the hot and cold feeling, which is an inability to control your body temperature, the shaking, the chest pain, the feeling of impending doom. Everything checks out. Talk to your PCP." He finished scribbling whatever it was he was writing down, then he ripped the paper off.

"I'm going to take this and give it to the nurse. It's a prescription for a strong anti-anxiety medication. It should tide you over until you can get in to see your regular doctor." He paused in the act of turning. Obviously, he had other patients to see. "Do you have any questions?" The brisk way he said it, and the way he was already turning away from her, made her think twice about asking anything.

"So there's nothing wrong at all with me?"

"No." He lifted his shoulder. "I can't diagnose what's not there. I know you're convinced you're having a heart attack, but from what I can see, that's not something you're going to have to worry about this decade."

Well, that was a little bit reassuring, except... "So it was just anxiety?"

"Yes. Long periods of stress often cause a person to have what might have been termed a nervous breakdown in previous years. It's a result of your nervous system being on high alert for far too long. It basically crashes and goes haywire, and you feel like your whole body is out of whack. It's what we've termed a panic attack."

"So what do I do to avoid them?"

He gave her a little smile, even though he was obviously in a hurry. "That's what I'd like for you to talk to your PCP about. They'll be able to give you all the details. For now, put yourself under as little stress as possible. Rest, eat healthy, and follow up with your doctor."

He paused, but did not ask her if she had any more questions before he turned and strode out the door.

"This is just anxiety?" Sasha said from the other side of the room.

Grace wondered why she had let her in there in the first place. She didn't need someone shoving her nose in the fact that she had canceled a sold-out concert that the president was attending in order to go to the hospital for a bad case of nerves. She was a professional. She didn't have bad cases of nerves.

Except, apparently she did.

"I'm sorry. I know I let you down. And all the people who paid to get in."

"Yeah. I told them you were most likely having a heart attack and you had to cancel the concert. I'm not sure I could tell them you had stage fright. Is that what we're gonna call this?"

"I guess it doesn't really matter what we call it, does it?" It was just a matter of her being too much of a coward to go out on stage and perform like she had been doing since she was a child.

"Well, I've told the president that we've rescheduled, and perhaps he will be able to make your concert next week. I suppose you're allowed to take one night off, although it would be nice if you didn't pick your sold-out concert, and the one where the president was attending. The concert last week made you a household name, and every concert between now and Christmas is completely sold out. You are going to do the concert next week, aren't you?"

Sasha must've finally noticed that she was being awfully quiet.

"I don't think I can," she said, and she didn't mean to sound fatalistic, but she could hear it in her voice. She really didn't think that she could. Not at all, and she wasn't the kind of person who spoke the word "can't". She believed, truly believed, that anybody could do anything that they set their minds to, except she had not been able to go out on that stage earlier this evening, and the idea of going out on it again was terrifying.

She had no idea what she was going to do.

Chapter Three

Candy canes twinkled from every other light post, while twinkle lights outlined large candles on the others. Grace's car slowly moved down Main Street in Mistletoe Meadows as she glanced at each shop, decked out for Christmas in a little over three weeks. It seemed like glitter was in the air, or maybe those were snow flurries.

She thought Virginia was supposed to be warm, not cold enough for snow. Especially not at the beginning of December.

But apparently she was wrong, because that was definitely snow coming down.

In the center of the town, the town square had been decorated to the hilt, just like everything else. A Christmas tree, huge and loaded with lights and decorations, dominated the area, although there was garland on the gazebo and shiny tinsel hanging pretty much everywhere.

Honestly, it felt a little overwhelming, as Grace's hands tightened on the steering wheel. The town even had Christmas music piped onto the street, that she could hear faintly through her closed windows. The current song was a piano jazz version of "Jingle Bells."

Even the sound of a piano made Grace's chest tighten.

She shook her head and glanced down the street, seeing her Aunt Vivian's Victorian home situated on the corner as it always had been during her childhood visits. She had garland hanging on the railing and wreaths in every single window, green with red bows.

It looked like there was a gingerbread house sitting on a table in front of the big picture window.

Grace glanced again as she pulled into the parking place right in front of Aunt Vivian's house.

Aunt Vivian had a small garage where she parked her own car off the street. Visitors always parked right in front, unless she was having a crowd, and then they parked at the church, which was just a block away.

Grace smiled at the memories. Aunt Vivian's beautiful, old, elegant Victorian house, bursting at the seams with friends and family and laughter and fun.

Invariably, since her entire family was musical, they'd end up around the piano. In the early years, Grace's mom played, but then, once Grace turned about seven, she took over the keyboard, and how she loved accompanying her musical family. Especially at Christmas time.

Even those happy memories made her stomach tighten and her throat close.

You have to breathe. The doctor said that it was all in your head. That you had thought yourself into it, and you would be able to think yourself out.

The doctor had offered her pills, but they were the kind of pills that once she started taking them, she couldn't stop. She had to wean herself off slowly, and she didn't want to be addicted to anything. Plus, everything that she'd heard from people who had taken the pills said it took the edge off, but it didn't cure anything. If she wanted to be cured, she had to do it herself. The problem was, she didn't know how.

So here she was, hiding out in the only place she knew. Aunt Vivian's Victorian house. She thought maybe the happy memories from her childhood would help with some of the issues, but she had forgotten that so many of those memories revolved around music.

As she got out of her car, she glanced across the street and up just a little bit. Connor's Music Shop, the same as it always had been, sat right there. It's where she had taken her first lessons and had fallen in love with the piano. She was the only one in the family, other than her mom, who played the piano. Everyone else played a stringed instrument. Her cousins had a string quartet that traveled the countryside, playing mostly folk and bluegrass, but also chamber music. They hired out for weddings and such. From what Grace understood, they made a pretty good living.

She was the only one who had gone solely professional, in New York City. She wasn't the only professional musician in her family, but, even if she were being modest, she was the best.

Or had been. Until whatever issue had gripped her mind had made her completely unable to perform.

She couldn't think about the entire month's worth of canceled concerts and accompanist positions. She'd even canceled her student lessons until after the holidays.

She'd hated to do that, but if she was going to leave the city, she hadn't had a choice.

She tightened her jaw, trying not to think about all the things that she'd left behind. The doctor had said that she needed to control her thoughts. She also needed to rest. They had suggested that maybe she had been working too hard, and she knew they were right. She had been working hard.

"Grace! I'm so happy to see you. I'm glad you made it safely."

Her Aunt Vivian stepped out on the porch, her arms spread wide as she hurried toward Grace.

She looked just as happy and cheerful as she always had, maybe a little older, more gray hair, more wrinkles, and perhaps a few more pounds around the waist and hips, but still her Aunt Vivian, still with a spring in her step, still with a love for her niece that made Grace think that this was exactly the right choice, even if some of the memories were going to be hard.

Chapter Four

Noah Connor clicked a few more things on his phone, sent a message to the group chat reminding everyone of the town meeting that evening, and then turned his phone off and set it down on the counter.

He glanced over beside his workbench, where a parade of instruments sat waiting for him to get enough time in his schedule to fix and refurbish them. Only one had an actual owner who was paying him to fix it. The others had been donated or found by himself or other people, for him to fix when he had time.

That wasn't really his first love, but sometimes it did pay the bills. He found that he could sell them online and make decent money as long as he didn't buy them for too much.

A broken instrument wasn't worth a whole lot, so he was usually able to get them at a pretty good price.

He pushed back away from the workbench and shoved his phone in his pocket.

He glanced in the back room, where students came for lessons, and where he had various instruments sitting on shelves for students to rent. He had an agreement with the Mistletoe school district that he provide instruments for their students at a reasonable cost.

He didn't make a whole lot of money on that either.

He sighed. There didn't seem to be a whole lot of money anywhere in owning a music store, but somehow his parents had made it work. Of course, forty years ago, music was a part of everyone's life, and typically they made that music themselves. Things had changed, everything had gone digital, and a person could play pretty much anything on any instrument from their electronics. Fewer and fewer people were learning to play an actual instrument. He wondered, sometimes, if it was going to be a lost art. After all, what was the point in learning to play an instrument if a person could just imitate the sound on an electronic device and have no need to put in the hours and hours and hours of work that it took.

There was no point in writing new music either, since a computer could do that just as well as a person also.

As was his custom, he went to the front door of his shop, but before he flipped the sign over, he turned around, bowed his head, and knelt down.

Lord God, thank you for this new day you've given me. Thank you for the music shop that my parents started forty years ago. Thank you that it has supported me and allowed me to raise my five siblings after my parents went to be with you.

Help me to be more like Jesus today than I was yesterday, Lord, and help people to see Jesus when they look at me. Bless my business, please, and help me to be a light in the darkness here in Mistletoe Meadows. Amen.

He kept his head bowed for just a few more moments. He never felt like he had enough time to tell God everything he wanted to. But, that was the most important thing, trying to be more like Jesus, so people could look at him and he would point them to the Savior.

That was more important than making sure that his shop remained solvent, more important than following his dreams, or doing what he had always hoped he would be able to do. He'd pretty much shelved all of those ideas and realized that his life really wasn't about him, it was about Jesus.

He pushed to his feet and turned around, flipping the sign so that it said "Open," and then standing and watching the traffic on the street. He loved this town, loved living in Mistletoe Meadows, loved being in charge of the Christmas festival, and loved that he had been able to keep his family together after his parents had died. Unfortunately, now that he had raised his siblings, and the last one had graduated from college, his job was over.

He went back to the counter where the cash register was and opened the drawer to get the cash box out.

His hand brushed a newspaper clipping that was old and yellowed with time. He stopped for a moment and stared at it. The title of the article was "Local Teen Wins State Competition," and underneath, the article ran down the side of a picture of him with his violin.

Funny that that article had managed to stay in this drawer all of those years. With the kids running in and out, and him working every day, taking the cashbox in and out.

That was probably Emma, making sure that the article stayed right there. She was the archaeologist in the family and was always trying to figure out what their ancestors were like.

He didn't reach back to the very end of the drawer, but he knew the unopened letter from the music conservatory in New York City was back there.

He didn't know whether he had been accepted or not, because at that point in time, his parents had passed away, and he knew that there was no way he was going.

Still, he'd never brought himself to throw the letter away. After all, at that point he'd already turned down the offer from Juilliard.

Pulling the cash box out, he shut the drawer with his hip and put it in the cash register as his phone buzzed several times.

Once he had everything organized and was ready for customers, he picked up his phone.

There were a bunch of messages on the family group text chat, and he opened it up. It started out with his younger sister Mia answering the question that he'd posed last night—who is coming to Christmas dinner, and what should he plan.

> Can't make it home for Christmas, sorry!

She didn't offer any reasons why, but he figured that the fact that she just started her new job in California probably had a lot to do with it.

His brother Jake said:

> New job demands crazy hours. Maybe next year?

He was going to text back that he was glad that Jake finally got his dream job, flying commercial airliners for a major US airline. He had been working his way up to that for years, and now had a route that took him from the United States to Europe to Australia, and every once in a while, he stopped off in Asia. He was definitely a globetrotter, although he'd been in the Air Force for years and had been stationed all over as well. It wasn't exactly new that Jake wasn't going to make it home. He'd probably only been home two or three times since he graduated from high school almost fifteen years ago.

From Emma:

> You know I'm not coming. I'm trekking down through Mexico and I'll be out of service for a while. Then I'll be thinking about you from the Caribbean.

Noah let the phone fall gently to the counter as he stared unseeing out the window.

He was pretty sure Cami wasn't going to come, since she was busy doing her residency in Houston, and from what he understood, the newer doctors got the worst hours. She probably wasn't going to get a single day off in the entire month of December and half of January.

And then of course, Cody wouldn't be home either, for whatever reason.

> I'm definitely jealous of the Caribbean. Enjoy yourself!

He hit send.

> Maybe you'll be in Australia over Christmas, and wouldn't that be fun to have Christmas in the summer?

He hit send again.

> Let me know how the new job is going.

He sent that one off and then allowed his phone to fall back down to the counter again.

No one would be home. He'd spent the last twenty years raising his siblings, and not a single one of them would be home for Christmas this year.

Was this how parents felt after their children had all flown the nest? This was the empty nest that so many adults dealt with, only he'd never been married. He'd been so busy raising his siblings that he hadn't even dated.

Not much anyway. The few times he'd tried, he'd scared his potential girlfriend away by talking too much about his siblings and what they were doing. That was his life though. That and the music store.

Well, he had one other thing he did, but no one other than his siblings knew about it. And even they didn't understand the extent that it mattered to him.

Typically, he didn't have a whole lot of business first thing in the morning, so he grabbed the window cleaner and a rag and walked over, squirting some on the big showroom window that allowed passersby on the street to look in and see the arrangement that he'd made with musical instruments and Christmas decorations.

He wasn't much of an artist, but he thought it looked pretty good.

He squirted some and began to wipe it off. Back when his siblings were home, each one of them had chores that they had to do in the morning, and for a lot of years, he hadn't washed the windows at all because it had been someone else's job.

But since Mia, his younger sister, had gone off to college, he'd been pretty much doing everything himself. He'd gotten used to only seeing his siblings sporadically, and the work of the music store sat on his shoulders alone.

How long was he going to be able to stay open?

He stopped wiping, and his eyes caught on the Victorian house on the corner. Vivian Dempsey was a lovely lady, and she had decorated her house beautifully, but that's not what caught his eye. There was a beautiful woman with long, dark hair washing the outside of Vivian's big picture window. The one with the Christmas town twinkling from inside.

The woman's hair shimmered in the morning sun, and as he watched, she finished wiping, stood back, and then turned around slowly and seemed to look right at the music store.

She had a graceful way of moving, and even from this distance, he could see that her hands and fingers were long and slender. Perfect piano-playing hands. Definitely musician's fingers.

He tried to think about who the woman could be. Maybe Vivian had hired a house cleaner, but he thought he'd heard something through the town grapevine about her niece coming.

Grace. He was pretty sure her name was Grace. He vaguely remembered his parents giving her music lessons several summers in a row back when they were small. She was a little younger than he was, but Vivian would walk her to the store, and his mom would take her to the back, where the piano was, and simple music would flow out for the next half an hour or forty-five minutes.

He'd not seen her often over the years, but... On a whim, he set his rag down and pulled out his phone.

He typed "Grace Dempsey" into the search bar, although he wasn't quite sure that was her last name. That was Vivian's last name, but maybe they didn't have the same one.

He waited for the page to populate, and then his stomach dropped as he read some of the headlines.

Musician Cancels December Concerts.
What Happened to Grace Dempsey?
Mysterious Illness Sidelines World's
Greatest Classical Pianist.

He stared at them for a while, and then looked back at the woman who had turned around and walked into the house, carrying her window cleaning supplies.

That long dark hair was pretty distinctive, and it matched the pictures that had come up for Grace Dempsey.

What was she doing in Mistletoe Meadows?

He shrugged it off, picked up his own window cleaning supplies, and walked out the door.

Chapter Five

"Would you mind picking up my prescription while you're out?" Aunt Vivian shouldered her purse and looked at Grace.

Grace suspected that Aunt Vivian was trying to get her to get out and meet some of the townspeople, but that was just pure speculation, since Aunt Vivian hadn't said anything of the kind.

"Sure," Grace said, not mentioning that she had had no intention of going out although it was a beautiful day and a walk would do her good. She knew it; she just didn't feel like doing it.

"Thank you. Dr. Hannah said that the sample for the new medication that I was thinking about starting was there, and I could pick it up anytime. I'll give her a ring and let her know that you'll be doing it for me." Aunt Vivian moved closer and gave Grace a hug, which Grace returned. "I'll be back by suppertime. Don't worry about doing anything. I'll stop at that really delicious sandwich shop on the outside of town and bring some subs back with me."

"Are you sure?" Grace said. "I can cook something."

"You're still settling in. You just take it easy and enjoy the beautiful weather. Pretty soon we won't have any nice days like this for a long time." Aunt Vivian waved her fingers and then disappeared out the front door.

Grace watched her leave and then glanced out the window. Aunt Vivian was correct, it was gorgeous out, and warm too. Unseasonably so for December. But that didn't make Grace have any more desire to take a walk. Although, if she took a walk, she could get herself further away from the piano in the parlor. She had shut the door to the parlor no less than four times this morning already, and somehow, Aunt Vivian always found an excuse to open it back up.

For some reason, just looking at the piano made her feel like she was going to have a panic attack.

Which, of course, brought back all of the feelings from the night that she actually had had a panic attack, thought she was dying, and... She didn't want to think about it. But there was no way she could even go in and sit down at the instrument, let alone think that she was going to play in front of any kind of crowd. The idea made her feel like she was going to throw up. It also made her heart feel like it was going to beat out of her chest, and her throat close and tighten.

She deliberately took a deep breath, closing her eyes and thinking about the beautiful, sunny December day.

Yes, a walk would be a great idea.

Grabbing her purse and a light jacket, she slipped out the front door and stepped off the beautiful Victorian front porch. She loved Aunt Vivian's house, and other than the piano in the parlor, it was relaxing and brought back happy memories of her childhood. Coming to Mistletoe Meadows was a great idea.

As she walked down Main Street, she was a little overwhelmed by the friendly greetings. She had forgotten just how friendly and happy the small town was.

After she had told at least ten strangers good morning and had a short conversation with three of them, she made it to the medical clinic.

It smelled like a typical doctor's office—antiseptic mixed with the smell of bandages and cleaner. The waiting room had a nicely decorated tree in the corner, and garland hung in loops the entire way around the room. The windows also had cute little Christmas decorations in each one of them. They looked homemade. Possibly made by patients, although Grace could not be entirely sure.

She walked up to the window and inquired about her aunt's medication. She fully suspected that she would not be able to pick it up herself, or would have to jump through a hundred hoops, but the receptionist smiled and said, "Dr. Hannah told me that you would be coming in. Apparently Vivian called. Such a sweet lady. She's your aunt?"

"She is," Grace said, looking at the name tag the woman wore. "Cassie."

"It's so nice that you're visiting her. Are you from around here?" Cassie's brows wrinkled. "I have to admit I haven't lived here that long. Just a couple of years, although I feel like I know everyone."

"This is probably a good place to work if you're thinking you're going to meet everyone in town."

"Exactly. Everyone stops by at some point."

Grace considered leaving the conversation at that, but she answered Cassie's question. "No. I visited here a good bit when I was younger, but I live up north."

"You're just visiting?" Cassie asked, not like she was interrogating her, but like it was a friendly question, and she was just making conversation.

"Yes. Just visiting. I'm not sure how long. I just needed a little break, and this is such a fun town. So many Christmas activities going on." She added that last bit to try to take Cassie's attention away from herself. It was refreshing for her to be able to walk around and have no one recognize her. Oddly, even though New York was a much bigger town, she was recognized almost everywhere she went and was used to people coming up to her and asking for lessons or pointers on their playing. She'd even had people ask her for references or to listen to them play so that she could recommend them to her agent.

She really wouldn't mind avoiding that kind of notoriety here.

Cassie chatted a bit, and then a young teen appeared at the back door to the little office area.

"Oh," Cassie said. "Mason will be bringing your medicine out, and he'll give you a little rundown on what your aunt can expect when she takes it." The boy disappeared from the back, and then just a few seconds later, he came out a door just to Grace's right.

"Hey there. I'm Mason," he said in greeting. He seemed very comfortable with talking to people, like it was something he did a lot. He also seemed very serious and into his job, more so than Grace would have guessed for a kid his age.

He went over the medicine very carefully, instructed her to tell her aunt to call if she had any questions, and then pointed to the number that was circled on the tag that had been stapled to the bag.

"Thank you very much, Mason," Grace said, impressed despite herself. The kid had a natural way about him, but she was sure, even now that she had seen him close up, that he couldn't be a day over seventeen.

Maybe that's what kids were like in a small town. She tucked that idea away. Having children was something she hadn't thought about much, since she had been so focused on her career. But, she supposed she wouldn't want to have them by herself. She would want her children to grow up in a stable, two-parent home.

She shook her head. When had she started thinking about children? And being in a stable, two-parent home?

Thanking Mason and smiling when he wished her a good day, she walked out, humming "Jingle Bells" under her breath.

It was almost impossible not to get into the Christmas spirit while walking through the town.

On an impulse, she crossed the street and ducked into Henderson's Candy Cane Shop that had been there forever as well. It was so festive and Christmasy, and so unique. She didn't recall seeing a single candy cane shop in the city, and she was curious since she couldn't recall - was the shop really all candy canes? The display in the window would seem to indicate that it was.

"Good afternoon," a cheerful woman said, looking up from arranging a display of raspberry-flavored candy canes. They were blue and pretty, and just one of the many candy cane displays in the store. It seemed like the store truly lived up to its name.

"Good morning. I had to come in and see a shop that was all about candy canes," she said.

"It's a little amazing, isn't it? Normally, my husband, Jack, is standing behind the counter making them. He happens to be off picking up his daughter right now, but if you want to see them created from start to finish, come back this evening." The woman smiled, genuine and friendly. "I'm Kate," she said, holding her hand out and tilting her head.

"I'm Grace. Vivian is my aunt. I'm here for a visit."

"I love Vivian. And her house is just amazing. That old Victorian, it's like eye candy. I look at it the way some people look at sunsets."

Grace laughed and felt a genuine bond with this woman, although they hadn't even been talking for five minutes.

"That's the way I feel. Living in it brings back all the great memories that I had growing up, and being inside of it is just as easy on the eyes as outside. Aunt Vivian has done an amazing job of decorating it."

"She usually has an open house during the Christmas parade, where people can stop in and grab some hot chocolate and look around. If I'm not mistaken, she spends several months making the gingerbread houses she has on display that night. I bet she's working on one right now."

"You would be correct. It's on the dining room table, and I have to say, it's coming together very nicely. She told me that I could try my hand at helping her, but I'm afraid of messing something up."

"I don't think that would bother Vivian. Everything seems like it's perfect, but she's told me several times about flaws in her workmanship. She just turns the flaws into beauty and makes it look like that's what she meant to do all along. I thought it was really clever," Kate said, laughing again with that infectious, cheerful, contagious laugh that made Grace smile.

"You are absolutely right. She taught that in life too. I remember her saying that when I was taking piano lessons from her years ago. If you make a mistake, just keep going. If you're practicing, you need to go back and correct it, but if you're performing, you just keep going and pretend like you meant to do it all along."

"It takes good acting I would imagine," Kate said, "although I don't play, so I wouldn't know."

"It's never too late to take lessons," Grace said automatically. She believed that. At any age, someone could learn to do something different. One didn't have to just assume that they'd missed out in their school years and could never break new ground and learn something new.

"You're right. Maybe I'll talk to your aunt about giving me lessons. Thanks for the nudge," Kate said.

They chatted a bit more, while Grace bought one of the raspberry candy canes, and then also a peppermint one, because she knew her aunt loved them. She figured it could be dessert after their meal of subs that evening.

With a promise that she would be back, she waved and left to the bell ringing over her head.

She almost missed the sign on the window down at the bottom, where it didn't interfere with the display.

She stopped, the smile on her face slowly fading as she read, "Thirty-year tradition—Annual Mistletoe Meadows Christmas Concert. Now accepting musicians. Practice every Monday and Thursday evening. Occasional practice on Saturday afternoons. See Noah Connor."

Noah's phone number was on there too, and for some inexplicable reason, Grace almost got her phone out and started to type it in. She stopped with a small gasp when she realized what she was doing.

No. No. She was not going to get involved in this small town's Christmas concert. What was she thinking?

Except... If she was playing along with a bunch of other musicians, maybe it wouldn't be so bad after all. Maybe she would be able to do that.

No. She came here to rest and recover. Not to bite off more than she could chew. Or to give herself another panic attack.

But she held her phone loosely in her hand, contemplating. Maybe it wouldn't hurt to take a picture of the flyer and think about it a little bit more. For some reason, she didn't get the panicked feeling in her stomach and throat the way she did when she looked at the piano in her aunt's house. Maybe she could do this. Except... Maybe they didn't even need a pianist. Maybe it was just stringed instruments... She glanced at the flyer again as she centered her phone. No. It didn't have any specific instruments on it. Maybe it just assumed that the people around town knew which instruments would be in the concert.

Snapping the picture before she could talk herself out of it, she tucked her phone in her pocket and hurried away, determined that she wasn't going to do anything to jeopardize her recovery, including playing in an annual Christmas concert, no matter how badly she was tempted.

Chapter Six

"The Mistletoe Christmas Festival is just one of the many Christmas traditions this town has. As you might expect because of the town name."

Grace sat in a chair in her Aunt Vivian's dining room, a blanket over her lap, knitting in her hands.

Her aunt sat across from her at the table, working on one of her intricate and exceptionally beautiful gingerbread houses. Just watching her aunt work made Grace feel relaxed and happy.

Soft Christmas music played from the speaker beside the window, and the occasional car drove down the street in front of the window, the headlights flashing.

The house smelled like cinnamon and yeast bread, and in the soft glow of the light on the coffee table, Grace could almost believe that they were in another world entirely.

The catastrophe of her last concert, the subsequent panic attacks, and fear that she might never perform again seemed like distant memories.

"I'd love to hear about them," she said, when Aunt Vivian didn't say anything more.

"Well, there's the Secret Saint. Our town is kind of famous for it."

"Secret Saint?" she asked.

"It's like a Secret Santa, only I suppose someone, I don't know who, coined the term, Secret Saint rather than saying Santa, because —and I'm just guessing here—a lot of times this time of year we get our attention off of what we're really celebrating and end up celebrating with the world. We even lie to our children and tell them that there's such a thing as Santa Claus, and make Christmas all about him and bringing toys and Rudolph and the North Pole. Sometimes we don't even bother to tell them the story of Jesus. Or, it takes second place to all the supposedly wonderful things that Santa does. Jesus can seem kind of boring after Santa."

Grace didn't say anything. She hadn't been brought up to believe in Santa Claus, and she didn't really understand why parents would lie to their kids that way. She was glad her parents hadn't, but she supposed it was a cute little story.

"I guess I don't really see anything wrong with Santa Claus, but I do agree that sometimes it feels like Christmas has been commercialized out of hand."

"I just think that's our little way of trying to make sure that we celebrate the true reason for the season."

"So what does the Secret Saint do?" Then she thought of an even more important question. "And who is it?"

"No one really knows. It seems to be different people. But whoever it is has a vast network of helpers who let them know when a townsperson might be experiencing difficulty or need some help."

"Like what?" she asked, curious despite herself. She'd never heard of a town that did this kind of thing.

"Sometimes it's simple things, like delivering groceries or a Christmas tree. Sometimes it's a little bigger, like giving a family who's had a hard time Christmas gifts to put under their tree for their children. Sometimes it's something as big as repairs to a home, like roofing or a new porch or fixing a banister. The list could go on and on. Sometimes the Secret Saint has paid off medical bills, given dental care to children, and even helped students with electronics and tuition bills."

"Whoever it is must know an awful lot about the town." It was too bad the Secret Saint couldn't figure out how to get rid of her panic attacks and help her overcome her stage fright so that she could perform again.

"That's why I sometimes suspect that it's more than one person. Or, maybe it's been multiple people over multiple years. I really don't know. And... I have been asked at times if I know anyone who needs help. I've been asked by different people, though, who claimed that they're not the actual Secret Saint but are just working as a network, and sometimes they even say that they don't know who the actual Secret Saint is!"

"My goodness. That sounds kind of complicated. But really, really sweet." It was so generous and kind that it made her feel really good to be a part of a town that had such a great tradition.

"It's definitely different, and sweet. You're right."

"Someone's sacrificing a lot. Whoever it is must be really rich."

"That's just it. I think it's the townspeople all donating together. It's not just one person funding everything. I could be wrong. Although, I've donated different things."

"I'm sure you have. You're always the first to help in an emergency."

"I try." Vivian chuckled a little and then shook her head. "If you want to know someone who is really good at sacrificing himself, you should just look across the street."

"Across the street?" Grace lifted her head, but she couldn't see much outside in the darkness. The street lights did illuminate the sidewalks, and the Christmas lights twinkled, but all she saw across the street was the music shop, which was closed for the night.

"Noah Connor. He owns the music shop."

"Oh, the music shop owner. What about him?" Grace asked.

"That man sacrificed a career like you have, only... Only we never knew how good he could be."

"What do you mean? Did he not have enough money to move to the city and audition?" She couldn't imagine how he could've sacrificed a career. Surely if he tried hard enough, he could've done the exact same thing that she did.

"No, nothing like that. His parents were killed in an accident when he was barely eighteen. From what I understand, he gave up Juilliard in order to raise the rest of his siblings."

"Juilliard?" Grace was impressed. "That's really giving up something if he had been accepted there."

"Yes. Someone needed to stay and take care of his siblings, and he was the only one who was considered an adult. The state would release them into his custody, but only if he stayed to take care of them. He stayed and ran the music shop. It was proven to have brought in an income, and he could hardly give up everything and run off to the city, where you know as well as I do, there was no guarantee that he could make money with his art."

The starving artist thing was real. She knew plenty of people who were just as talented as she was and who worked just as hard, but who hadn't gotten the breaks that she had. Not that she felt that she owed her success to luck. Not at all. She had worked hard, she had developed the talent God had given her, and she had been in the right places at the right time. It sounded like this Noah person could've had the same thing happen to him, only he could never be in the right place, because he was staying home taking care of his siblings.

"Couldn't he have asked Juilliard to allow him to wait a couple of years and then use his scholarship?" she asked.

"He had a lot of siblings. In fact, he is your age, and the last one just graduated from college this spring. I'm pretty sure his Juilliard dreams are over and out. But he seems happy and content."

Aunt Vivian sounded a little bit unsure about that, and how could she know?

There was something in her tone that caused Grace to look up at her. Was her aunt lonely? She had never even considered before that her aunt might be anything but exceptionally happy in her beautiful Victorian home with her very full and productive social life. It seemed like her aunt had her fingers in everything and was constantly helping people. And she mostly seemed happy. There was just something in her tone... But it was gone. Still, the idea wouldn't leave.

"Are you ever lonely?" She didn't know how else to ask the question and just allowed it to come out the way it needed to.

"My goodness, child. What a question."

It wasn't Grace's imagination. Her aunt paused in squirting icing on a piece of cinnamon candy before she began working again. "I think everyone has times where they're down or a little upset. I wouldn't be human if I didn't. But, I've had a good life. A great one. God's been so good to me. What more can an old lady ask for than to have her niece come visit her and sit and knit in a cozy living room on a cold December evening?"

"It is pretty nice, isn't it?" she said, glancing at her aunt before looking over at the Christmas tree that twinkled in the corner.

If she wasn't here, would her aunt be sitting in the living room alone? Would she be sad? Would she be wishing that she had someone to share the evening with?

She sensed there might be more to her aunt's story, but she didn't push.

Her aunt was one of the best Christians she knew, living out her faith, not just saying what she believed, but actually living it too.

It seemed like everyone in the town did that. Maybe not everyone. There were always people who allowed the bad to be bigger than the good in their lives and in their hearts, but... A town that had a vast network of people who helped a Secret Saint bring comfort and joy to so many of its residents had to have a lot of good people, who didn't just talk the talk, but walked the walk too.

She was definitely interested in spending more time with the people. Maybe some of their faith would rub off on her. As it was, she felt a little bit at loose ends.

Lord, what am I supposed to do with my life if I can no longer perform? I thought that was the way I used your gift. But now... Now my fingers are silent, and I feel like I have no purpose. I want to serve you, Lord. But how?

Chapter Seven

Noah's fingers flew across the keys as he finished the prelude, and the pastor walked to the pulpit.

Because of the position of the piano in the church, it was easy for Noah to look out over the congregation, which he mostly avoided doing. Years ago, they had set the piano in this position so that he could keep an eye on his siblings while he was playing. As his siblings got older, the position of the piano had stayed the same, although he didn't need it. They had all learned quickly that Noah would take care of things at home if they misbehaved in church. And then, thankfully, they had gotten to the point where they wanted to behave themselves in church because they were interested in what the pastor said and wanted to become closer to God and learn more about the Bible.

Thank you, Lord, that so far, all of my siblings are following you.

He was so grateful for that. He would've felt like he'd failed his parents if the devil had gotten a hold of any of them and they had walked after the flesh rather than the spirit.

Of course, their lives weren't perfect, but no one's was.

As the pastor greeted the congregants, Noah's eyes swept over the congregation, and then, without really meaning to, they got caught on a woman in the back pew, sitting beside Vivian.

Grace Dempsey.

She was just as regal looking as he remembered.

He was a little embarrassed, because he knew how well she could play. He'd seen YouTube videos and videos of her on social media, and she was amazing. And there she was, sitting in the congregation, listening to his pitiful playing.

No, he knew he was an accomplished pianist, although he was better on the violin. He might not have made it to Juilliard, but he had spent a lot of time practicing. One of the benefits of owning a music shop. All of his siblings had learned to do their schoolwork while he played in the background.

Still, he was nothing compared to what Grace was, and he felt like he didn't belong on the bench as long as she was in the congregation.

He tore his eyes away in time to hear the pastor announce the first hymn, and thankfully, he had already turned to the correct page in the hymnal. All he had to do was set it in front of the music that he'd used as a prelude. Of course, he could play the hymn by heart, as he could almost every hymn in the hymn book. He'd played them enough times. Sung them even more, had all the verses memorized. In fact, sometimes he felt like the hymns in the book had more doctrine in them than many of the so-called religious books that were published nowadays.

Because he knew the music so well, he was able to look up and glance around the congregation, although he didn't make a habit of it. Still, he couldn't seem to keep his eyes off of Grace.

His fingers almost stumbled, and he only caught himself because of years of muscle memory, when he realized that Grace was crying.

At least it seemed like she was wiping tears from her eyes as they sang "What a Day That Will Be."

He did a run on the right hand, accompanying with chords on

the left as the congregation swelled in harmony, lifting glorious music to the rafters and beyond.

Music always made his heart feel big and his soul expand, and this was no different. But crying?

He supposed he could understand how hymns might be a little sad.

Unfortunately, as they sang two more hymns and finished the opening part of the service before the pastor began his message, he noticed that Grace cried through all of the music.

Was his playing that terrible?

It made him doubt himself a little, but he thought that it was more likely that whatever was going on in her life had affected her, and the hymns, which truly did have deep doctrine and truth, probably reached to her soul and pierced her heart.

He wanted to go back and comfort her, which was an odd feeling, and he attributed it to the empty nest syndrome, which had made him a little uneasy, feeling like he didn't quite have his equilibrium back. It was weird to be alone, and he certainly had comforted his siblings more than once. The girls especially. They seemed to get upset over everything, but he didn't recall any of them ever crying while singing hymns.

To his surprise, as the last verse of the last hymn before the sermon drew to a close, he noticed Grace standing and slipping out the back.

What happened? Was it truly that upsetting? Was there some kind of sin in her life that she felt guilty about?

If it had been his sister, he would have left the piano bench after the hymn and gone out to see what the problem was.

But Grace was still a stranger to him, even though he felt like he knew her after his Internet search, and there was something intriguing about her on top of that. But, she was still a stranger, and he tried to put her out of his mind as he sat and listened to the pastor deliver an excellent sermon.

Still, as he got back at the piano to play softly for the altar call, he couldn't stop himself from glancing back to see if Grace had returned.

She had not.

He couldn't stop his mind from wondering where she had gone and what her issue could possibly be, but he was jolted out of his thoughts as the pastor finished the service and then reminded everyone of the town business meeting at the town community center that afternoon.

It wasn't necessarily church business, but the church and the town were so intertwined, and the people who ran the town were also heavily involved in the church.

At least it gave him something to do this afternoon. Since his siblings had left, he had imagined himself finally relieved of his duties and enjoying the time alone. But he found instead that Sunday afternoons, especially, were long and seemed to drag on forever. His silent phone, with no texts or calls from his siblings, reminded him that he was no longer a necessary part of their lives, and while he knew it was a natural thing, he was a little sad. It made him sad to think of all the years and time that he'd spent, and now, he was alone. By choice, he supposed, since trying to date while running the business and giving private lessons as well as raising his siblings was just too hard.

He forced the gloomy thoughts aside and played something perky and relevant to the sermon for the postlude as congregants filed out. Playing the piano always made him feel better, and just because he was enjoying himself, he played a second song as the last of the people lingered, chatting and socializing.

Still, as he finished up and carefully closed the piano, gathering up his music, he couldn't help but think about Grace. What had been wrong with her?

Chapter Eight

"You'll have to try some of this, it's delicious." Roland McBride held up a spoonful of what looked like a fajita soup. "I've gotta get the recipe for this." He mumbled as he nodded and then walked away.

Noah grinned. It was a little hard to imagine Roland cooking. But he knew the man did. He'd seen his dishes at church potluck suppers and different community events over the years.

Roland had been a bit of the black sheep of the McBride family, but he'd settled down in the last few years, and no small part of that was because of his wife, Nellie.

Noah glanced between the two of them as Roland insisted his wife try some of his soup, holding up his spoon and waiting for her to open her mouth.

She looked long-suffering as she did so, and then her eyes opened wide, and apparently she liked it.

Roland became animated, and the two of them turned together and walked toward the refreshment table.

Noah grinned and then looked down at his own plate, devoid of any soup. Maybe he should've tried some.

He supposed if he went back up, he would. But he'd been keeping an eye out for Grace. He kind of hoped she'd show up.

Everyone who attended had brought a little something to eat, which Noah appreciated. Now that he was on his own, regular meals were almost a thing of the past. What was the point in cooking for just one?

He pressed his lips together and tried not to go down that rabbit hole. He'd get used to it. Plenty of people lived by themselves and were completely content. And he'd done it for years almost, since his youngest sibling had gone to college and had only been home on weekends. Still, while they were in college, he still felt responsible and had regular phone conversations with them over friends and grades and work. Not like now, where his job was basically over.

He chatted with a few of the townspeople who walked up to him before it was time to call the meeting to order.

He always ran the meetings, or at least got them started. Today he didn't have a whole lot to do, because the committees would be giving their reports.

Just as he was walking up to the podium, his phone dinged.

He glanced at Dr. Terry Landis, looking tired but exceptionally happy as she snuggled her newborn baby, with her husband Judd's arm around them.

They were talking to Marjorie McBride, who sat in a chair with a blanket over her lap. She looked thin and frail and much different than she had even last year. Whatever health issues she was fighting, she apparently had not overcome them.

He'd been praying for her on a daily basis, both morning and evening. She was such a pillar of the community, he couldn't imagine life in Mistletoe Meadows without her.

He was a little distracted, thinking about Marjorie, as he glanced at his phone, and then, he had to slow down and read again to fully understand what was going on.

His stomach dropped, and dread felt like a lead vest sitting on his shoulders.

How was he going to tell the town this?

"We gonna get started?" someone asked, but Noah barely glanced at them and couldn't say who it was. He needed to think. There had to be a way to figure this out.

But he didn't have time. He needed to get the meeting started, and he would have to present this to the community without a solution of his own. This wasn't the kind of news that could wait.

As he looked up from the podium, he was surprised to see Grace standing in the back.

So she came after all.

His eyes wanted to linger on her, to see if she was okay after the emotional time she'd had in church, especially with the music, but he didn't have that kind of luxury. He had to get the meeting started, and no one else was going to do it for him. Somehow, he always seemed to land these roles. Taking care of his siblings, leading the community in whatever project they were doing, and even with his newest, most secret job. Somehow the mantle of being in charge of that had fallen on his shoulders.

He glanced at Roland. He could thank his friend for that.

"Welcome everyone. If everyone could quiet down, we'll get started. You can keep eating though. I have it on good authority that the fajita soup is delicious."

A murmur went through the crowd, and Dr. Hannah Reynolds grinned. He suspected the soup was hers, especially when Ben Tucker, town policeman who was also in charge of the security and health committee along with Hannah, bent down with a grin on his face and said something in her ear.

She beamed even more.

"I'm just taking a wild stab, but I'd say it's Dr. Hannah's. So that means it's probably healthy too. If there's any left after the meeting, you better grab some."

A couple of people got up at that moment, which was fine. People didn't need to sit in chairs the entire time he was talking. Everyone was always respectful and quiet, and that was all he needed.

Although, he wouldn't mind a distraction right now. He hated to have to bring this up to the town, but they might as well get started on it first.

"Normally I let all the other committees say their piece first, and I report last, but I just got an email that I feel needs to be addressed immediately."

He didn't mean to pause for dramatic effect. His pause was more to figure out how exactly he was going to say this to his community. The people he worked with. The people he loved and who put their heart and soul into the Christmas festival every year. After all, when you live in a town called Mistletoe Meadows, you could hardly not do Christmas big.

"I just got an email from the band we put a deposit on. We went a little wild and crazy on this band. They're nationally known, and we booked them almost two years ago, since this is our thirtieth Mistletoe Meadows Christmas Festival, and we were going extra large."

They'd had so many hopes and dreams, and so many of them were hinged on this band.

"Bottom line, they're not going to be able to make it." He didn't need to say exactly why. They could talk about that if they wanted to. Here was the information that really mattered. "They say that we're not getting our deposit back."

A murmur went through the crowd. But, for those who didn't know, he felt like he needed to continue. "It was far more than what we usually pay. About 75% of the Christmas festival budget. We were planning on this being a major, major moneymaker for the town and for it to more than cover not just the fee for the band, but the entire budget for the Christmas festival." He could feel the tightening in his chest. The anxiety that squeezed his stomach. He knew he would get calm. He always did, but he hated that he had to say this. "Needless to say, we're in a really hard spot financially with the Christmas festival. Not only are we losing 75% of our budget with apparently no hope of getting it back, although I will definitely be having a lawyer look into this, but we also are not going to have the income that we thought we were."

"Unless we can replace it with something else," Jones Quebedeau said.

There was a murmur of agreement.

"I just got this message literally as I was stepping up to the podium. I have no suggestions, but I am definitely open to ideas."

There was more murmuring as people chatted amongst each other. His eyes swept over the crowd, and they landed on Grace. She was looking at him, but as their eyes met, she yanked hers away and turned immediately, heading toward the door and walking quietly out, slipping quickly away.

He wanted to leave the podium and go after her. But this was where he belonged. He had responsibilities, and he couldn't just leave them. Maybe some people could. But that was how he had ended up raising his siblings. Because someone had to take responsibility for them, and that seemed to be him.

"What do you think the chances are of getting that deposit back?" Wilson McBride, standing with his wife, Charity, asked over the din of other voices chatting amongst themselves. Everyone quieted as they heard his question.

"I have to be honest. I'm not sure. They said in the contract that we had agreed to a nonrefundable deposit. But, the way I think these things usually work is it's nonrefundable if we cancel. If they cancel, we get a refund. But this is not really my area, which is why I said I would be having a lawyer at least look into it. If it seems like it's worth pursuing, I hate to go that route, but we're talking about a lot of money." But now he had to say the kicker. "But that's not going to happen overnight. These things take time, and I would be willing to bet it'll be a month, two, or even a year until we see any money back. So, for now, we need to plan the Christmas festival as though it's not coming. And then, we need to do everything we can to make sure we get it."

Wilson nodded, and Jones, who was standing right beside him, said, "I have a good lawyer. If you need me to get him to look at it, I can. I'll pay for it too. I get that we need to come up with a different idea for our festival, but we also don't want to just lose this money, to roll over and take it if they owe us our deposit back."

"I agree completely, and I will get your email address later and forward the contract and the information to you so you can take it to your lawyer tomorrow."

"I'll be on it first thing," Jones said with a nod of his head.

His wife, Amy, who used to be a McBride, looked up and smiled at her husband. The smile held worry and concern, though. Which was not the way Noah wanted the Christmas festival to go. He wanted people to enjoy it. To have a good time. Not to worry about financial things.

"We have been hoping to have the biggest and best Christmas festival ever, to celebrate thirty years. Lack of funds is going to really put the kibosh on that," Jack spoke. His wife, Kate, sat right beside him, and their daughter, Lilly, who was deaf, sat beside them. Kate automatically translated everything into sign language for Lilly.

It seemed like everywhere Noah looked, there were couples. Deeply in love couples who stood side by side and weathered storms together.

Lord, where's my mate? Where's the person who will weather storms with me?

Not for the first time he thought about being a single parent. Even then he wouldn't have minded if God had sent him someone, but he hadn't had time to go look for her himself, and God had not dropped her into his lap.

Still, even though this was not the time, he couldn't stop the longing that went through him. He wanted someone to walk through life with side by side. Someone who smiled at him and got his inside jokes. Someone who encouraged him when he was down and who looked to him for encouragement when they needed it as well. He wanted that sharing of ideas and of smiles and secret jokes and shared laughter. A companion across from him at the supper table, someone who inspired him to get back to having regular meals.

Where did all that come from?

He was in the biggest catastrophe that he'd handled so far as the unofficial chairman of the Mistletoe Meadows Festival committee. He needed to focus.

"Maybe we should do some other business and give ourselves a little bit of time to think about ideas," Wilson McBride suggested. His wife, Charity, also stood beside him, but Noah did not allow himself to be sidetracked back into that spot where he wished that he had someone like that. It was awfully close to coveting, although he didn't want Wilson's wife. He just wanted to be someone who had a wife beside him.

"I think that's a great idea. Maybe we could even shelve it for a day and convene tomorrow when we've had time to think."

"Yeah, I like that idea."

They voted on it and everyone agreed this was something they needed to move on, but also needed to think about.

"Alright, that's taken care of for tonight. Ben, are you and Hannah ready to give the report on the security and medical committee?" he asked, and Ben and Hannah nodded together, holding hands as they walked to the platform.

Normally Noah stood off to the side while committee reports were given, but this time he stepped completely off the podium. He didn't realize he was doing it until he continued to walk to the back door and slipped out.

Having the big band that they had booked two years ago cancel on them at the last minute had been a huge blow. He'd thought he had everything well in hand, but this made him doubt that he was even fit for the job. Of course, it wasn't his fault and he knew that. But he couldn't help but remember that he had talked everyone into booking this big-name performer to draw people in and making a big deal about their thirtieth Mistletoe Meadows festival. If he hadn't done that, they wouldn't have lost so big.

But, nothing ventured, nothing gained. As a business owner, he knew that risk was an integral part of growing. A person couldn't grow and develop without taking risks of some kind. Whether it was a financial risk or a personal one.

He was being too hard on himself.

Although, he didn't really know much about personal risk, not when it came to romantic relationships, except he had bet on his siblings when he'd given up so much in order to raise them.

He supposed that counted.

He had only intended to go out for some fresh air, but the town square and gazebo faced the side door where he had slipped out, and he could see long dark hair and a purple hat he recognized.

Grace had gone over and stood at the entrance to the gazebo, leaning against one of the pillars and watching the ducks on the pond.

He probably had ten minutes while Ben and Hannah gave the report and had a discussion. He hadn't intended to be gone all that time, but he found his feet taking him toward the gazebo.

Such a talented musician, so much beautiful music came from her fingers, and she was here in this town. Sure, he was a little starstruck, but also concerned. Was she okay?

It was the protective instinct that had enabled him to raise his family, that had wanted to pull everyone close after his parents died and continue to be together. After all, that's what families were for. And, he believed he had been successful. His siblings were all close, even if they weren't home, and everyone got along with everyone else, which was better than eighty percent of the families that he knew.

But he wasn't patting himself on the back, because he'd spent a lot of time on his knees, asking for God's favor and help. If he had been successful, he knew the credit all belonged to the Lord.

Still, he had made the choice to give up a career and possibly a relationship in order to do what he knew God wanted him to do. And he'd do it all over again, although he was lonely.

Grace heard him as he approached the last five feet, and her head turned, her eyes widening in surprise.

He couldn't tell if she had been crying, but he wasn't really looking for that. He was caught by the vivid blue of her eyes, which contrasted nicely with her dark hair. And maybe brought out a little by the purple of her hat. Her cheeks were rosy, and her lips full, and they turned up in a little smile.

"I'm Noah Connor," he said, holding out his hand.

"Grace," she said. He noticed she didn't include her last name.

He thought about letting it go, but he wasn't going to pretend that he didn't recognize her.

"I thought so. Grace Dempsey, famous concert pianist."

Her face pinched, and her hands, which had been warm and squeezing his, pulled away quickly.

"Yes," she said, and then turned away.

"I know who you are, but that's not why I came over to talk to you."

"Oh," she said, as though it didn't matter, her shoulder lifting.

"I just noticed that you seemed a little upset. I thought I would come out and check to make sure you're okay." That hadn't really been his plan consciously, but he realized subconsciously that was exactly what he had planned to do. She had been on his mind since he'd first seen her crying during the first hymn that morning.

"I'm fine. I just needed a little air. I don't really have anything to do with the festival anyway. I was just there because my Aunt Vivian invited me and said that was where we were going to get fed. I felt a little out of place."

"I think if you give Mistletoe Meadows a chance, you'll find we're a very welcoming town. You don't have to live here for thirty years before you're allowed to contribute to whatever we're doing, whether it's a festival, or a church service, or anything." He paused for a moment. "If you'd like to play the piano while you're here, you're certainly welcome to."

"No."

He closed his mouth. Surprised at her quick and sharp retort.

She seemed to soften a bit, and her head tilted. "I'm sorry. I didn't mean to snap. But, you did a beautiful job this morning. The music... I haven't heard hymns played with such passion and feeling in a long time. It was beautiful. No one else could possibly do it as well as you can."

"I wasn't really thinking about you doing it better. I just know that you can. And the offer is open."

"I won't be taking you up on it, but thank you."

"No pressure. But my door's open if you change your mind."

His siblings had always made fun of him for carrying around business cards. He had tried to tell them that one never knew when the opportunity would come to give someone information, and what might come of that simple gesture. He'd tried to teach them to always be prepared. As a business owner who struggled year after year, trying to raise five children on what amounted to a little bit of nothing, he certainly had taken his own advice.

At this point, he thought maybe it had paid off finally, since he was able to reach into his shirt pocket and pull out a business card. He almost laughed at himself. This wasn't really what he wanted with Grace, but he couldn't quite put his finger on exactly what it was. There was something about her that had intrigued him from the first time he'd seen her in person. Of course, he knew of her and had heard recordings of her playing. But, this was different. This was personal.

But he couldn't let it be that way. He held out his card. "Feel free to call me anytime."

She looked at the card, and then at him, and then back at the card.

White fingers, slender and cool, with short nails that would not interfere with her piano playing at all, reached up and took hold of the card. There seemed to be a pause, although it could've been his imagination, before she took it and said softly, "Thanks."

"I need to get back."

He didn't want to leave.

"I know. You were leading the meeting. You probably shouldn't have left." She paused for a moment, and then she said, "The soup was really good."

His eyes shot to hers in surprise. She had been listening. He grinned a little, and she returned his smile with a ghost of her own.

"Yeah. Come back and get some more."

There seemed to be something shimmering in the air between them. Something sweet and precious, but he didn't have time to search it out. He had to get back.

"Maybe," she said.

She gave no other promises and looked away from him, back across at the ducks that frolicked in the small pond.

He couldn't think of anything else to say and felt a little foolish as he turned around and walked away.

Chapter Nine

Grace stared at the book. She had been trying to read for the last fifteen minutes but she hadn't turned a single page and could not tell what the book was about.

She snapped it shut, heaving a sigh of frustration as she put it on the coffee table.

Feeling restless, she pushed out of the chair and wandered around the room. It seemed so empty and cold when she was here by herself. Aunt Vivian had an appointment and had politely declined Grace's offer to go with her.

Grace hadn't wanted to insist, and she definitely didn't want to admit that she didn't want to be at the house by herself.

There were too many things to think about, and she didn't want to think about any of them. She wanted to be distracted by something.

Her eyes lifted, and she looked across the street to the music shop. No. She didn't want to be distracted by just anything. Noah was not a good distraction.

But she couldn't help but remember the kindness in his eyes as he'd spoken with her the previous day. She had seen him coming, and for some odd reason, her heart had given a couple of extra beats in her chest. He wouldn't have been considered handsome by any of her friends in the city, but he looked rugged and capable. Like someone she could depend on. Someone who would take care of her. Someone who would protect her and consider it his duty to be the head of the home.

She didn't know how she could tell all of that by looking at him, but it was that feeling that she got, one of safety and security when he stood there in front of her. She didn't even know she wanted that, but she had been drawn to it immediately.

She fingered the card that she had stuck in her pocket. She had put it on her nightstand the night before, and then on a whim that morning, she'd picked it up and stuck it back in her pocket. She'd been touching it all day. It was almost as though touching the card brought back the memory of Noah more clearly and distinctly, and she could feel the warmth and security that she'd felt while he stood in front of her.

Another student carrying an instrument case, most likely a violin, walked into Noah's store, passing a student on their way out.

That was the third or fourth student she'd seen that day heading into Noah's store. There had been several over lunch as well. Like he taught an ensemble at that time.

He must give individual instruction. She thought he would be a great teacher. That he would push students, but not so hard that they got discouraged.

Suddenly, thinking that the kitchen had a window with a slightly different angle of the music store, Grace hurried from the living room and walked down the hall into the kitchen.

She didn't stop to question herself about why she was so interested in what Noah was doing, but instead, went to the window and angled herself over the counter so she could see the music store.

Sure enough, she could see the window of the back room, and the student setting their instrument case down and getting it out, and Noah saying something, causing the student to laugh.

He seemed like he was so good with them.

As she stood there, the lesson began, and the student did well at first, but then came to a passage they struggled with. Noah seemed encouraging, considerate, even getting down on one knee at one point and pointing to the music, and then picking up his own violin and playing. Then, in a gesture she easily understood, he encouraged the student to try again.

He was so good with kids. So kind.

She blew out a breath and pushed away from the counter, knowing that she would be embarrassed if her aunt walked in at that moment. She would want to know exactly why Grace was stretched out over the counter, craning her neck around so she could see something. Her aunt would think it would be something exceptionally interesting. Not a music teacher giving lessons.

Grace glanced at the clock. Another hour until her aunt got home and the book club met.

She remembered she was supposed to make brownies and hurried to get the ingredients out and throw them in the oven. She'd been so distracted by Noah that she'd totally forgotten.

She couldn't do that. Noah was just a man like any other, one of thousands she'd met over the years. She knew that a lot of times the best musicians made the worst teachers. But, Noah was obviously a good musician, and he played at least two instruments quite well.

She made a mental note to ask her Aunt Vivian about him if she could. Although, she didn't want to bring any attention to her interest in him, since she knew her interest was slightly more than normal.

Not in a bad way, not in a romantic way, just... an interested way.

She had no other words other than that.

At five o'clock on the dot, Nellie McBride and Kate Henderson were at the door. Aunt Vivian had gotten home thirty minutes prior and they were ready for their company and the book club discussion. Cassie, the medical clinic receptionist, came in slightly later.

The five of them settled down in the living room with a tray of brownies and several other finger foods the ladies had brought. Each of them held a copy of a book, *Heartland Joy*, by an author that Grace had never heard of.

She hadn't read the book, so she listened to the conversation as her aunt gently guided it.

"I thought the most powerful moment in the book was not the romance, but was when Shaun knelt by the coffee table and prayed with a child that wasn't even his." Aunt Vivian opened the conversation.

Nellie nodded. "That was powerful. Especially because I think as a parent, my first instinct is to defend my child and to attack anyone who attacks them. I definitely don't automatically go to the biblical passage where we're supposed to love our enemies and pray for those who persecute us. I might think of that for myself, but not for my children."

"Exactly. But how are our children supposed to learn if we don't guide them in that direction? If we hold them to a different standard than what we hold ourselves?" Kate asked.

"Sometimes I think we hold our children to too high of a standard. But in this case, it's a biblical standard, and biblical standards are not too high." Cassie weighed in.

"It's funny how we want all the best for our children, and a lot of times we feel like that means veering away from the Bible and giving them material things." Aunt Vivian sounded wise.

"I agree with that, although that reminds me that the music teacher at the school quit just a week ago, and now there's no band concert, and I know children at the school are bitterly disappointed. I mean, you practice all year, and you think you're going to enjoy getting to play for an audience, and then it doesn't happen." Kate sounded dismayed.

Grace kept her mouth closed tightly. She had benefited immensely from playing in orchestra when she was younger. Perhaps she would not have been a concert pianist if she had not had those opportunities. They had given her a taste of something she loved and made her realize that it could be something that she could do with her life, although she knew that she would have a lot of work to put into it. Perhaps she wouldn't have worked as hard if she hadn't known that. And then she wouldn't have made it.

Guilt stirred in her heart. Those kids needed someone, and she had the ability to step in. Maybe she couldn't be hired as their teacher, but she could at least volunteer to help them get music together for a concert.

She noticed her aunt giving her a look, and she noticed the look being shared among the other women.

They all knew who she was and what she did for a living. Perhaps that's why Kate had brought the information up.

But the women were kind and gracious and did not push.

"We probably should get back to the book. We're not doing it justice. I was definitely convicted over the prayer, and I do believe that's probably the most powerful moment in the book, but the half haircut made me chuckle for a really long time." Grace was grateful to Aunt Vivian for changing the subject. She wasn't ready to put herself out there again just yet.

The other ladies started to laugh. "I can imagine my husband walking out of the barbershop with half his hair chopped off. That was hilarious."

"The romance was really sweet too. It wasn't too much, but it was just enough to make your heart flutter a little."

The ladies kept talking, and Grace listened in. But, in the back of her head, she was still thinking. Could she? Could she get the kids together and attempt having a concert?

She'd never done anything like that. She'd participated in plenty of them, and she had taken classes on conducting. She could probably get music. She had connections, and she also had her own abilities. She could rewrite music to make it simpler if necessary. Or transpose according to the instruments they had.

But she didn't say anything, and the book club broke up after two hours.

"If you don't mind, I'm gonna take a quick walk," Grace said to Aunt Vivian after they had cleared the living room and done the dishes.

"I don't mind at all. I was on my way to take a shower, but I'll be back down in the living room in a little while."

"I'll meet you there." They smiled at each other, and Grace again got the idea that Aunt Vivian was lonely. She seemed happy for the company anyway.

Putting her coat on and pulling her purple hat down over her forehead and ears, she shoved her hands in her mittens, wrapped her scarf around her neck, and walked outside.

It wasn't as bitterly cold as she'd expected, even though the sun had gone down, taking its minimal warmth with it.

She walked along the street, thinking, trying to keep her mind off of the idea of the band concert, but she found herself crossing the street and heading over to the music shop. She wanted to be like a child and stick her nose on the glass and peek inside, but she didn't. Instead, she stood there, and in the quiet, she heard the most beautiful violin music drifting through the cool night air.

It wasn't anything she recognized, although there were plenty of symphonies where she didn't know every single part of every single instrument. Still, this sounded like a melody, and one she should know, except she didn't.

As her eyes got used to the dark, she realized Noah stood inside, his back toward her, a small light behind the counter casting a glow up on his face that she'd missed because of the glare on the window from the Christmas lights behind her.

It was even more obvious when he stopped playing, bent over, jotted something down, and then began to play again. He played with so much beauty and emotion, his tone so clear and pure, but he was clearly playing for himself and not for any kind of performance. But... When he stopped again and jotted something else down, and then went in a different direction, she had to wonder...was he writing his own music?

Almost as though he finally felt her eyes on him, he turned, still playing, and looked out the window.

For a brief, frozen second, their eyes met. His music stopped mid-note, and he was obviously embarrassed.

Grace was embarrassed to have embarrassed him and to have been caught staring and putting her nose in his business.

She mouthed "sorry" before she jerked back away from the window and hurried away.

For the first time since she'd come to town, she prayed for God to show her what He wanted from her, instead of her begging God to do what she wanted.

Lord, is there a reason for me being here? Is there a reason for everything that I'm experiencing? Do you have some kind of plan that I'm not aware of? Is it for those children who need a band concert instructor? She paused, and then she gathered herself and said, "Please, Lord, show me what you want, and then give me the courage to do it."

Chapter Ten

Tuesday morning, Noah sat behind the counter, his laptop open, inventory up, when the bell over the door rang, and a man he did not recognize walked in.

As a music store in Mistletoe Meadows, he occasionally got people from the surrounding countryside who were looking for a music store but didn't want to make the two-hour drive to a larger city, and would stop in here first.

Whatever he didn't have, he could order, but usually what they wanted was advice and his thoughts. After all, whatever they wanted, they could also order now. It didn't used to be that way, and while it was better for the consumer, most likely, it had certainly hit his pocketbook hard.

Still, he dispensed his advice as liberally as he could, hoping that he was giving the best advice possible.

But this man... There was something about him that made Noah think that he wasn't here to purchase anything or to ask for advice.

"Noah Connor, I presume?" the man said, holding out his hand.

Noah stood up, since he'd always been taught that one did not shake hands sitting down. "I am. And you are?" he asked, still a little put off by the man's demeanor somehow. He tried to shake that. He would be polite and friendly to anyone.

"Name's Rick Hastings. This is a cute little shop you have."

"Thanks," Noah said, somehow thinking that the man didn't mean it as a compliment.

"Business good?"

"It's okay," he said, more defensive than he meant to be. He wasn't going to talk about his business with a complete stranger.

"Well good, good. This is a quaint little town. Did you grow up here?"

"Yes I did. I raised my siblings here as well."

He tried to find neutral ground, and appreciated the man doing the same. He could talk about Mistletoe Meadows. He was not going to talk about his business. Not when he didn't know anything about this fellow.

"Well, I'll just level with you. I represent Moondoes Coffee."

Noah kept his face passive. It was a chain coffee store, every store like every other store, and it was a knockoff of several other more popular, more personal chains. The idea that the man was here announcing that made Noah want to scratch his head, but the man wasn't finished, so he kept his mouth closed.

"We're interested in putting in a store here in Mistletoe Meadows. I wanted to come in person and offer you a cool six figures to purchase your shop and the building, since we're going to tear it down and put a store right here on Main Street. Because of the industrial park going in outside of town, we see it expanding by at least fifty percent in the next two years, and that's a conservative growth estimate. The festival here in the winter and the Christmas in July festival you do as well are both huge draws, and we figured out that we can make a lot of money here."

"I'm sure you probably could," Noah said.

"Great. I brought a contract with me today," Rick said, setting his briefcase down on the counter and beginning to open it.

"You don't need to do that. The shop was my parents'. It's all I have left of them. I'm not selling."

"Are you telling me you're making enough money to be able to turn down a very good six-figure offer?" Rick asked as he pulled a stack of papers half an inch thick out of his briefcase and set them on the counter. "This is the contract."

Noah stared. He had signed contracts that were less than a page long. They probably wouldn't hold up in a court of law, but those were the kind of contracts that he liked, although he liked even more to just shake someone's hand and know that their word was as good as his.

He understood that wasn't the way business was done anymore, but he liked the idea. The contract was off-putting. But, the man was right. Six figures was nothing to sneeze at, and he would never have an offer that good again.

"If you'd like to sign now, you certainly can, or, I can leave it here. I have the authority to give you twenty-one days to look at it."

"Twenty-one days?" Noah said. That wasn't even a month.

"Yes. That puts us..." Rick pulled out his phone and pulled up the calendar app. "Right at Christmas Eve. You can let me know then, or anytime in the meantime. Once the offer expires, we're going down to Whisker Hollow at the base of the mountain, and we already know we can buy a building there." He looked around, and Noah thought he read disgust on the man's face. "But we prefer this location. Not necessarily this building. It looks to me like we'd be doing the town a favor to tear it down."

"Passes inspection every year," Noah said, trying not to sound defensive.

"All right, well let me know. Offer expires December 24th." Rick tapped the top of the paper, gave Noah another look, and then walked off, the cheerful bell ringing behind him at odds with the sick, curling feeling in Noah's chest.

He should sell. He should. That would be the wise decision.

He swallowed, checked to make sure Rick was gone from sight, and then gathered the contract up and put it on the shelf behind the counter to look at later. He'd probably read through it, although it looked like a lot of legal mumbo-jumbo that would make sure that every "i" was dotted and every "t" was crossed for the good of Moondoes Coffee. If Noah decided to sign, he probably should hire a lawyer of his own. Jones had said he had a good one on Sunday at the meeting. Maybe he would have to talk to Jones.

He still had the contract and the offer and the idea that he wanted to reject it on his mind when Mark Stevens, his best friend in the world, walked in the store.

"Hey there," he said, smiling for real for the first time since Rick had darkened the doorway.

"You look terrible," Mark said, coming over and shaking his hand before going to the coffee machine to pour himself a cup. It was something that Noah had started keeping in the shop as his siblings got older and could drink it. They all enjoyed it, and none of them liked going back upstairs to make it in the morning. In fact, for a while, when everyone was in high school, they had cooked their breakfast on a hot plate in the store as well.

"I've had better days." He lifted his shoulder. He and Mark had a lot of other things to talk about. Mark was a pastor in the next town, although Noah was hopeful that Pastor Johnson would retire and Mark would take his place. Of course, Mark would say that he wasn't going to do anything without feeling like God wanted him to do it, particularly take on a different church, but Noah still held out hope. Mark was a perfect pastor for their town, other than the fact that he wasn't married. Noah had a feeling that a lot of the women would prefer that he have a wife, because typically the pastor's wife ran a lot of the ladies' programs at the church. She could be a real asset, but not if he didn't have one.

Mark was also his partner in the Secret Saint venture that they had taken on.

"I was out last night delivering the groceries like we talked about. And I heard some more things after church on Sunday that I wanted to go over with you."

A lot of people from Mistletoe Meadows went to Mark's church, just because Mark was such a great pastor and had amazing sermons directly from scripture. Pastor Johnson was excellent, but he was getting older, and some people preferred a younger, more energetic man.

Noah loved Mark, but Pastor Johnson was an excellent pastor, and he didn't go to or leave churches lightly. He had zero plans to leave, as much as he would love to support his friend.

"Okay, that's great. I coordinated getting a new roof for Mrs. James' house and replacing the shutters and painting the front porch on the Jackson property."

"Awesome. Here are some things I found out on Sunday."

They leaned over the list as Mark went over it. Noah had some ideas, and he also had some contacts he could get ahold of to help donate. After they'd looked it over and talked about it for a while, they figured out how to take care of the entire list.

"And, I heard that the music teacher at Mistletoe Meadows High School quit."

"She did."

"I know this isn't something we usually take care of, but those kids would really like to have a concert."

"Normally they practice for months beforehand."

"They would have the music that they've been practicing. We just need someone to direct it."

"I suppose so."

"What about you?"

Noah blinked. He hadn't thought about that at all. He... wasn't really qualified.

"I don't have any formal training. I don't really know how to read music scores, and that might involve transposing and that type of thing. Nothing that I know anything about."

"You write music on the side."

There weren't a whole lot of people who knew that. Mark was one of the very, very few.

All of a sudden, Grace's face came into his mind. The surprise on it when she'd seen him, the knowledge that lurked in her eyes, that he could see even in the dim light from the street lights. She knew. She knew he was creating his own music as well.

"I'm just not qualified."

"I figured you would say that. But I actually happen to know that you have someone in your town who is qualified."

Noah paused and then nodded. "We do." He didn't think she would do it though. She'd shut him down immediately when he had asked about playing the piano in church. Something was going on with her, and while he hadn't found out what, he was sure that she would reject Mark's suggestion.

Plus, he had the Mistletoe Meadows festival to think about. He was directing the adult music for that, and it was totally missing their headlining act.

"I heard about the festival," Mark said, as though he were reading his mind. Good friends often were like that.

"Yeah. We decided that we would go home and think about it for a little bit after we threw some ideas out that just didn't seem quite right. I don't know what we're going to do."

"Are you gonna get your deposit back? When I was talking to Blanche, she wasn't sure."

Mark referenced one of the older ladies who lived in Mistletoe Meadows but went to Mark's church.

"I don't know. Jones called his lawyer yesterday, and of course, you know how that goes. The lawyer is gonna get back to him eventually, but probably not fast. So I'm pretty confident that we are not going to have the deposit in time to use it for this year's festival." That was a real downer, and he didn't want to end on that, so he said, "But I'm pretty sure that everything else in the festival is going really, really well. I'm so glad that Ben and Dr. Hannah got together. They are doing a phenomenal job with their committee, and it's not costing us one red cent. They've managed to get donations to cover everything. I wish all the other committee heads were that inspired to save money."

"Well, you know, music happens to be your thing. And, an original composition might be just the ticket."

"Nobody wants to hear my stuff," Noah said. He'd submitted it often to different publishing houses and professional orchestras and other groups. But no one was interested in playing it. And he'd never had the money to hire someone to play it and record it for him. Not that he'd ever had any compositions that he thought were good enough to warrant such an investment. He knew that a person had a tendency to be unable to judge the quality of their own work.

"Just do me a favor and think about it. You know it wouldn't hurt you to put yourself out there a little bit. Your siblings are gone, and taking a little bit of a risk isn't going to hurt anyone."

"Except for me."

"God has you. Pray about it. Because I'm pretty sure that God did not say, 'Okay, you're done raising your kids, now you can rest on your laurels and do nothing with the rest of your life.' You're done with that portion of your life. See what God has for you next, and shine."

Noah rolled his eyes at Mark's cheesy words, but he understood exactly what Mark was saying, and Mark was right.

Chapter Eleven

That afternoon, Noah left the shop for a little while after lunch so he could deliver the Secret Saint items to Mr. Peterson.

"You said this was from who?" Mr. Peterson said, leaning on his cane at the front door, looking at the bag of items that Noah carried in each hand.

"The Secret Saint. He's an anonymous person who donates to folks in town around Christmas time. You've heard of him."

"I sure have. But I don't understand how he knew that my children were coming in to eat, and I didn't have a lot of money to spend on groceries. How did that happen?"

Noah shrugged, waiting patiently until Mr. Peterson had rolled things over in his mind long enough, and then realized he was standing in the doorway.

"I'm sorry. I didn't mean to be rude. Come on in."

"Thanks," Noah said, walking into the house. The living room was covered in photos of Mr. Peterson's late wife, who used to be the pianist at the church.

Maybe Mr. Peterson noticed Noah looking at the photos. "It sure upset me when I heard that we weren't going to have the community Christmas concert this year. My wife loved them so much, even the concerts that were a monthly thing there for a while back in the day. People gathered in the square, and I remember seeing it filled with people standing shoulder to shoulder, enjoying the music on the stage. My wife lived for those things. She picked the most popular music, and there was always some kind of spirit behind her playing, whatever it is that makes people sit up and listen and want more."

"I remember. She was really good, and I loved sitting in the yard. My parents would always do a picnic in the summer months. It was something we would look forward to for weeks prior."

"Me too. It's too bad they went the way things go. I guess that happens. Progress and change, they say. I don't know that I call it progress as much as I call it regress."

Noah had set the bags on the kitchen table and got the cold things out so he could set them in the refrigerator.

"People carry their music around with them on their devices now," Noah said, knowing that Mr. Peterson probably had an opinion about that. But that was why live concerts weren't really a thing anymore. That, and there weren't a whole lot of people who were learning how to play instruments anymore either. After all, why did one need to do that when, with a touch of a button, a person could have any instrument they wanted playing in their ear.

"That's sad. There's just something about a live concert that brings the community together. It gives everyone something to look forward to and a reason to gather together and talk to each other. We don't do that anymore."

Noah nodded, glad that they had brought the groceries, since Mr. Peterson's refrigerator was completely empty, other than a jug of milk that looked like it might have expired the week prior.

"It used to be that people loved doing those kinds of things. Anymore, all we do is go to sports games and watch people chasing a ball around on a field. Where's the class in that? It doesn't appeal to our higher side, it doesn't lift our spirits and bring glory to God. It's just a bunch of men grunting around."

Noah might not have agreed completely with Mr. Peterson, but the man was entitled to his opinion. And he was right about the arts being good for people and elevating them. Music did that in a way that he couldn't really explain.

Still, as he left Mr. Peterson's house and walked slowly back to his store, which he hadn't bothered to close—he'd just put a sign on the counter that said "Will be back in ten minutes"—he thought about how right Mr. Peterson was, and how... Maybe he could create something even better than what they used to do. Then it would be progress.

Chapter Twelve

Noah sat at his piano, the last piano student gone for the night. It was late, and he should go upstairs to bed. When his siblings were home, he'd kept a strict "no one up after midnight on a school night" schedule. But now that they were gone, he found himself wandering the house in the evening, or, more likely, doing what he was doing now—sitting at the piano, allowing the melody and the harmonies in his head to dance around, singing, playing, and capturing it all on paper.

There were programs that allowed a person to compose based on what they played on the piano. The computer would transpose and put the notes that were played on a staff. But Noah preferred to compose the old-fashioned way. It was in his head, teased out by his fingers, and then written down and fleshed out on paper.

He hummed the bar, then hit a few piano keys, adding a little embellishment, before going back and changing it a bit.

Then, another voice chimed in. They teased back and forth, like a conversation, a flirty one.

It went on like that for a long time, as he took the music down, completely in the zone. By the time he was done, he realized he had been writing music for a violin and piano when he had been intending to write a piano composition.

He looked at the melody carried by the violin, and then picked up by the piano while the violin added depth and harmony.

He'd never tried to write a duet like this before. He had written some compositions for the violin to play with piano accompaniment, and even more compositions for piano itself, since that was the more popular thing if he were trying to sell it, but this... This was something completely different.

He looked over the music, hearing it in his head, humming along a bit, and felt satisfied.

Then a thought came to him as he closed up for the night.

Was he writing this for Grace and him to play together?

Immediately he knew it was true, even while most of him wanted to deny it. He wasn't thinking about Grace the whole time, not consciously, although ever since he'd first seen her, she was in his subconscious all the time. But he hadn't intended to write this for them. The one time he'd asked her to play, she'd said a short no, and there was obviously something bothering her, plus, she was a famous musician at the top of her game, and he was an unknown in a tiny town in rural Virginia. There was no way she was going to play one of his compositions, and she certainly wasn't going to play with him.

He tried to put that out of his mind as he tidied up the music room, getting ready for lessons the next day. He did miss his siblings, because they'd helped with that. Almost always one of them would have the room swept and dusted while he finished up lessons. But he wasn't overwhelmed by the work.

With all the things going wrong, he still hadn't figured out a solution to the issue of the Christmas festival music, and he hadn't heard back from Jones, which he figured was not a good thing.

Plus, what Mr. Peterson had been saying to him about the music that used to be in town on a monthly basis had been on his mind. He was the music store owner. Was it his job to keep music alive in the town? Of course it would benefit him, but maybe he'd just been too busy with his siblings and trying to keep the business going and the lessons that he did on the side to earn enough money to buy groceries, that he hadn't thought about it.

But yeah, he would be the logical one. Either him or the music teacher at school, who had left abruptly, and in a way he supposed she'd left him holding the bag. All of the music in the town was on his shoulders.

Maybe not, but it felt that way.

Lord, I feel overwhelmed. There's so much stuff coming at me. All of the music issues, plus the money issues, plus the offer I have on the store. It's tempting. It would take away a lot of my worries and allow me to do things I've always wanted to do, but haven't been able to, either because of money or because of raising my siblings, which I appreciate the opportunity to do, but... I gave up a lot. I didn't really see it as giving up anything though. I wanted to.

Help me figure it out. Help me do what you want me to do.

He needed wisdom and discretion. To know what to do.

Maybe he should just give up on the idea of music altogether. Because, after all, what he'd said to Mr. Peterson was correct—people carried their music around on their devices anymore. They didn't go see people perform live. Even churches were giving up on live music and playing canned stuff, or having a band on stage playing music that anyone who knew three chords and had fingers could play. He didn't disdain that type of music. It was simple for a reason, to make it accessible to every church anywhere, even if they didn't have accomplished musicians. But that was just the thing. His church did have an accomplished musician. Or at least a musician who could play whatever was set in front of him for the most part.

But that wasn't really the pressing problem. Not like the issue of whether or not he should accept Moondoe's offer, or even more pressing, what he should do about the Christmas festival and the music there.

An idea started to come to him, and he tossed it around. Maybe it wasn't a terrible idea. Maybe he could do something along those lines. It wouldn't cost any money. Or at least it shouldn't cost much. And that would be the best thing, since the finances of the festival committee were really low, thanks to the fact that they might not get their deposit back.

Maybe God had orchestrated that all along, because He had something else in mind.

Lord, help me to do what you want. Give me wisdom to know what that is.

Chapter Thirteen

race strolled slowly down the street of Mistletoe Meadows. As had become their custom, while Aunt Vivian showered, she took a walk. It was funny how people settled into a routine, and it felt good and cozy and right.

Ben Tucker, the deputy sheriff, strolled by and tipped his hat at her, offering a "good evening" which she returned.

Funny how friendly small towns could be. Especially to someone who barely knew anyone.

As she walked by the clinic, Hannah glanced up from chatting with a patient and threw a hand up in a wave and a greeting.

Grace waved back, loving how people were friendly but not too intrusive. Sometimes small towns could be rather overbearing, or at least she'd heard that they could be. Her friends from small towns had complained about them at times in the city.

It was interesting. She didn't really miss her friends too much. Maybe she missed Katrina a little. She had been her best friend in the city. But she supposed she hadn't taken the time to cultivate a lot of friendships, since she'd been so busy practicing and working.

As she got to the music shop, she slowed, automatically drawn to it. It was the music, not Noah, she told herself as her feet came to a stop at the door. Remembering what had happened the last time she had been peeking in the window, she noted the time, that it was still open, and pulled the handle, walking in.

It was like walking into a place that felt very much like home. There were instruments on the walls, guitars and banjos, even a couple of violins and a viola. The place smelled like rosin and wood, with a faint hint of a man's aftershave, not too strong, and a perfect mix with the other music smells.

"So you're not going to watch from the window tonight?" Noah said, straightening up from behind the counter where he must've been kneeling.

It was a gentle teasing, and she smiled. "I'm sorry. I... I guess I'm drawn to the music, and... You were very good." She wanted to ask if it was an original composition, but she didn't.

"Let me show you around a bit. You're welcome to try out anything you'd like. And I'm not saying that as a salesman. I'm saying that out of respect for your great talent and ability."

He seemed sincere, but she didn't really want him to think of her as someone who he was a fan of. She wanted to be friends. She wasn't sure what it was about him, but the same way walking into the shop felt like home, being in Noah's presence felt like safety and protection, and she felt secure and unafraid in a way that she'd never felt around anyone else.

"You'll recognize the Fender guitars. These are used, which are actually more expensive than the new ones, because these were made before they started making a lot of things overseas."

"Yeah. There are some good quality things coming from the East, especially in keyboards and pianos, but guitars just aren't what they used to be." She wasn't an expert in guitars by any means, but she knew enough to know that a used guitar was definitely worth more than a new one. For now, anyway. She ran her finger gently over the cool wood as Noah watched with a half smile on his face.

"There's an aura about instruments that I love."

"How many do you play?"

"Just the piano proficiently. I could probably pick out maybe three chords on the guitar."

"Enough to play most Christian songs that are sung in church," he said with a grin.

She realized he was laughing a bit. "Yeah. That's why they make them that way, right? So anyone, including me, could play."

"I think so. There are good messages in some of them though."

That seemed to be a concession. She got the distinct feeling that he didn't think much of some of the music that was in churches at present.

"Do I detect a little bit of music snobbery?" she asked.

"Maybe?"

He didn't say anything more, but from the twinkle in his eye and the self-deprecating smile, she imagined that he knew he was a bit of a snob. She thought it funny that he didn't apologize for it, though.

"I give lessons back here. You probably haven't seen that."

"I've noticed kids coming in and out. Most of them carrying instruments. Do you rent them?"

"Yeah. I have an arrangement with the school. Although with the music teacher gone, a lot of the kids you saw coming in and out with instruments were probably kids that were coming to return them, since there's no point in them paying rent when they're not taking lessons."

"The music teacher at the school?" she asked, although she already knew it. She assumed they would fill the position immediately.

"Yeah. A couple of weeks ago. It's too bad, because people were looking forward to the Christmas concert, and the kids, especially. They put so much work into learning to play the instrument, and then it's a real letdown to not have any place to show off what they've learned."

"Yeah. That's too bad. It's too bad that someone couldn't at least take over and help the kids."

"I agree."

"How many instruments do you play?" she asked, thinking that teaching the kids was something that he could do, too.

They had stopped beside the piano, and she touched the side of it, feeling a slight unease, but not the full-blown panic that she had grown used to. For some reason, Noah's piano didn't inspire the fear that her Aunt Vivian's did.

"I play two proficiently. Piano and violin. Obviously, I'm not as good at the piano as you are."

"Most people aren't," she said absentmindedly, pushing down on one key.

The sound was perfect, but it also jarred and scared her. She yanked her hand back.

Then she was embarrassed at her reaction. She took a breath, blew it out, and then lifted her gaze to meet Noah's. He was studying her with hooded eyes.

"Something happened to you."

It was a statement. Not a question, and she looked away. Maybe it was his comforting presence, maybe the feeling of being in the building full of instruments and music and the joy and laughter and uplifting feelings that evoked for her, or maybe it was just the man and how he felt like safety.

"You don't have to say anything." But he left the comment open-ended, like she could if she wanted to.

"I don't know what happened at my last concert. I was in the dressing room, thinking about going out, and all of a sudden, I thought I was going to die. It ended up being a panic attack, terrible, terrible stage fright, which I've never experienced before. I mean, I've performed countless times, all over the world, and I've never had anything like that happen to me before. But it's been debilitating. Even looking at a piano is enough to make my stomach twist and my throat tighten and I feel like I can't breathe."

"You just touched one. Played a note."

"I know. It... isn't as bad here." She almost said "with you," but she wasn't sure if that was it or not.

"I wonder why," he said.

"I'm not sure. The doctors said there was nothing wrong with me physically. They recommended I go see a psychiatrist, which I did a couple of times, but I felt crazy, you know?"

"So you came here, thinking maybe that would help heal whatever was wrong?"

"Yeah. I suppose. Or maybe it was just I didn't know what else to do. Playing in front of anyone wasn't an option when I could barely breathe even looking at a piano, let alone the idea of people listening to me."

"That's why you refused me when I asked you if you wanted to play for church."

"Yeah. I'm sorry. It was kind of you to offer, and normally I would've loved to. Hymns are my favorite, and there's just something powerful in the words and the melody together. I could be transported away for timeless moments and come back, not just having enjoyed the music, but having had a little sermon all at once, just because of seeing the verses in my head."

"Hymns are special that way. So many of them are based fully on the Bible. Not that modern music isn't. Some of it is."

"That's okay. I already know you're a snob when it comes to Christian music."

Noah looked a little embarrassed.

"So you must be getting better. Here you are, touching a piano."

"Aunt Vivian has a piano and I can't go near it."

That didn't mean anything necessarily, other than Noah could be right. Maybe she was getting over it. Or maybe it was him.

"I'm sorry. I didn't mean to dump all my problems on you."

"I asked. I was curious. I knew that you had canceled your last performance, but there's no other information on the Internet at all, and I didn't know." He took a breath and then he continued. "And, just so you don't feel left out, I've been struggling a little bit myself.

Not necessarily with music, but my parents died when I was eighteen. All of my siblings are younger than me, and I was the only one who had the option to be the guardian, otherwise they were going to farm us all out to foster homes. So, I gave up my music career to take over the shop and raise my siblings. I've never regretted it, but now that they're all gone, the last one graduated from college, I just feel a little... Not sure what to do. None of them are coming home for Christmas, so that's new, and... I guess I feel like I have an empty nest, and in reality, I don't even have children. I just have siblings."

He looked like he hadn't meant to say all of that, but she'd been listening intently, and he'd continued.

"I can't imagine what it would be like growing up with so many siblings. I was an only child."

"That would've been terrible. Although I guess you would've had all of your parents' attention."

"Yeah." It wasn't quite that way, but she wasn't going to get into that now.

Instead, she read between the lines. "You gave up your music career to raise your siblings."

"I didn't have a music career. I guess I gave up the possibility of one."

"I bet you did a really good job." She looked at him thoughtfully. He just seemed like the protective older brother who would be perfect for that role. Interesting how God worked things out exactly the way they should be. But she could feel the sacrifice Noah had made.

"I don't know about that. They're all pretty much self-sufficient."

"And following the Lord?"

"Yeah. First and foremost. Following God."

"Then you were a success."

They looked at each other, and something seemed to pass between them. Something that she couldn't put a name on, but that felt like an understanding that they both had.

"So I have an idea," Noah said, and he sounded a little hesitant.

"Okay?"

"What if you and I worked together on something small, music-wise."

"What do you mean?" she asked, expecting to feel her chest tighten, but it hadn't. Not yet.

"I mean the kids need someone to help them practice and prepare for the Christmas concert they were planning on giving. I know that the groundwork is laid, but they need us to come in and finish. Do the planning, make sure everything comes together. That type of thing."

It wouldn't require her to play anything. She would just be helping kids, which would be a good thing. She thought about the kids that had been in and out of the shop that week. Children who could possibly be professional musicians one day, if someone took an interest in them. Her childhood might not have been perfect, but at least she had been given the opportunities that she had. If these kids didn't have someone come and continue to teach them, they might not have those opportunities.

"I've got to be honest, the shop will benefit some, if the kids continue to rent the instruments from me. But that said, I charge such a tiny amount that it really doesn't cover much of anything other than the instrument purchase and the insurance I have to pay in case they break it."

"Of course. I would want your shop to benefit in some way, if at all possible. I know that making a living as a musician, and I would assume as a music store owner, is not the most lucrative, nor the easiest job in the world."

"It's not. But somehow I managed to raise all my siblings on it, and my parents had been doing it before I took over. I would say that's more God than any kind of economics."

"God is good. That's for sure."

He nodded in agreement.

"What do you say?" he asked, and there was hope on his face.

She thought about the kids she'd seen through the kitchen window, eagerly practicing their music, struggling with a scale, and Noah's calm and patient attitude with them. She thought about how people had helped her and how much she had enjoyed her career until it had been cut short. Maybe doing this would help her get back on track too. And, working with Noah might help. He made her feel calm and grounded in a way that she didn't with anyone else.

"Let me think about it," she finally said.

He nodded. "That's fair. Let me know when you make a decision, please. No pressure, but we are running out of time."

"You're right. I won't take very long." Realizing that a ton of time had passed, and she had intended to be back before her aunt was done with her shower, she turned and started toward the door.

"I'm sorry. I didn't mean to take up so much of your time. I better head back."

"No bother. Come back anytime. I mean that."

She stopped and turned. Everyone in town had been exceptionally kind to her, but there was just something about Noah. His offers were sincere, and she knew that when he said he didn't mind, it was true. Plus, she felt drawn to him. And, to be honest, she didn't want to leave.

"I know you do. Thanks." Before her feet could do something different, she forced them to turn around and head toward the door. She did not look back as the bell rang above her and then the door closed. Somehow, as much as she would like to work with the kids and knew that that was good, and as much as she thought that it might be helpful to her in getting over her stage fright, the draw of working with Noah was more than any of those things.

Lord, I want to do what you want me to do. Please give me wisdom to know what that is.

Chapter Fourteen

Noah pushed the pan sitting on the floor in the hall over just a bit, so the water leaking from the roof would hit the center of it. He had emptied it when he had gotten up that morning, and it was currently only a quarter full. It would probably be fine until the rain stopped later that day.

As he got up to move away, he heard the furnace kick on, doing some kind of rattle and bang that had gotten worse in the last two weeks. A new roof, a new furnace. What else?

That six-figure buyout from Rick Hastings of Moondoes was looking better and better.

He sighed, going back down the stairs and heading out to the shop. He'd already opened it, but had wanted to run upstairs and check the pan to make sure it wasn't overflowing. There wasn't much point in catching the water if the pan overflowed.

He had his phone out to check to see when the rain was going to quit, or to see if it was going to turn to ice and snow, when it rang in his hand.

His brother Jake came up on the caller ID.

Maybe he'd changed his mind about Christmas. Noah answered more eagerly than he expected to.

"Hello?" It wasn't that Jake never called. He did. But, he supposed anytime his siblings called, he worried that something had happened.

"Bro, how are you?"

"I'm good," he said, a little uncertain. Jake sounded rather chipper. Like he wanted something and was buttering Noah up.

But rather than ask "what do you want," like he might've done back when Jake lived with him, he decided to take a slightly more diplomatic route and instead he responded with, "How are you doing?"

"I'm doing great, but I met this girl."

Noah's heart leapt. He was eager for his siblings to get married, to have children, for them to bring them around and visit more. Maybe that wouldn't happen if they got married, but he was hoping.

"Really?" he prompted.

"Yeah. She's in a pretty bad way. She had the transmission go out in her car right in front of my house, and I know that God sent her here for a reason."

Noah couldn't argue that was sometimes the way the Lord worked.

"But I can't afford to replace her transmission, and neither can she. So I guess I was wondering if I could borrow five grand from you. I promise I'll pay it back. But I just want to do a good deed for her. She's got two little kids, and... She could really use the help."

All of his extra cash had been tapped out for Secret Saint things, and the only thing he had was his emergency fund, which is where the roof repair and the furnace replacement was going to come from. If there was enough in there to cover that. But he had about $500 more than his brother was asking. And it wasn't even a debate in his mind.

"I'll write you out a check and send it to you, unless you want to come pick it up."

"I don't want to take off work. There's some overtime I've been picking up, and if I'm gonna be paying this back, I'm definitely gonna need it. The garage has agreed to fix it, and it's going to take a week. So if you drop it in the mail today, I should have it in plenty of time."

"I'll do it."

"You're the literal best, Noah. Thanks. I know that no matter what happens, I can depend on you."

"Hey, that's what brothers are for," he said, even though he never felt like Jake's brother. He'd always felt like his dad, or at least, since his parents had died, he'd felt that way. Even beforehand, he had been the responsible older brother, always looking out for his siblings.

He hung up the phone after saying a few more words to his brother and stepped out into the shop, which was empty. Not unusual for this time of the morning. Although, sometimes at Christmas, it got a little busier as parents bought guitars and cases and music for their children to put under the tree.

It happened less and less every year. He sold less and less every year, but he still considered this season his best, and the rest of the year was based on what he made now.

But sales were down, he had the repairs looming over his head, now his emergency fund was wiped out, and it felt like the noose was tightening around his neck. Still, he did not hesitate, but grabbed the checkbook to his emergency fund and started writing out the check, grabbing an envelope and addressing it to his brother.

Maybe he should take that buyout. Maybe that was the best thing to do. He didn't really feel like he was letting his parents down exactly. He was sure—as sure as he could be—that his dad would say that if it was no longer making money, he should sell it. It hadn't gotten to quite that point, but definitely profits were down, and he wanted to get out before he was in the red and ended up upside down. But, this was where he and his siblings had grown up. It was where he had the most precious memories of his family, both the ones that were with his parents and the ones after they passed. There was so much laughter, so much shared music and fun and song. They used to have variety shows after the store closed at night in the summer. Just him and his siblings, putting on things to make each other laugh or to impress each other with their abilities. He couldn't imagine not getting up and standing behind this desk, facing the town. And that was another thing. The town. The people, his neighbors and friends. He loved it here. He really didn't want to move to the big city anymore.

He stopped for a moment. Was that true? He had been thinking about restarting his career, but... His dreams had changed. He no longer wanted to be a famous musician. He just wanted to serve the people of his town, the children who needed a concert director, the kids who came for lessons, the parents who came to him for advice on what guitar was the best one and what music should they buy and what piano course did he recommend, plus he played for church, and he had the Secret Saint.

He didn't want the buyout. He didn't want a lot of money that promised to make his life easier but would just take away the things that he loved.

At least he didn't think he did, he thought as he heard the water dripping above his head and the furnace kicked off with a clang and a bang.

One of these days, it was going to kick on and no heat was going to come out. And then he was going to be in a pickle, because... He looked at the check in his hand. There went the money to repair it.

He shoved it in the envelope, grabbed the stamp from the drawer, and set it on the counter to give to the mailman when he arrived.

Yeah, his life had problems, but whose didn't? And sure, money would solve the problems he had, but then he would end up leaving everything he loved.

Lord? What should I do?

Chapter Fifteen

Grace walked slowly beside Aunt Vivian to the community center building, where the emergency Christmas festival meeting was taking place.

"I sure hope someone has come up with an idea," Aunt Vivian said, sounding worried. It wasn't like Aunt Vivian to sound worried, and that made Grace's stomach twist.

"I can't think of a single thing," Grace said honestly.

Aunt Vivian gave her a look. "You mean you don't know anyone who could provide music for the town festival?" Her brows were raised, and her tone said that everyone knew that she knew someone.

"Me?" she said.

Aunt Vivian just arched her brows.

"You know why I'm here," she said softly, looking around in case anyone was watching. But no one was paying them any attention. Most people on the sidewalk were going the same place they were and weren't close enough to hear what they were talking about.

"Your name would bring people from all over. Not just this

locality. It would be a nationwide thing. They would be overrun with guests. So many they probably couldn't handle them all."

Grace didn't say anything. Aunt Vivian was probably right. They wouldn't be the usual festival crowd, but they would be there just to see her, and the town would make money from it, but... She wasn't exactly the kind of person who played at festivals. Beyond that—it wasn't that she was too snotty to do so. The problem was, she hadn't played since that disastrous concert that she had to cancel, and she didn't know for sure that she could do it.

"I don't want the entire town depending on me to pull this off when I don't even know for sure that I'll be able to play. I don't want everyone to be disappointed. I don't want to let them all down. They're too important to me."

Her aunt didn't say anything, just nodded and continued to walk.

Grace held her tongue and didn't argue anymore. Her aunt knew she was right, but she also knew that her aunt was right. All she had to do was say that she would give a concert, and they would have more people there than they ever had before for anything. She might even outdraw the big-name band that they had hired that canceled.

But she couldn't do it. She couldn't take the pressure, couldn't stand the idea that if she failed, everything failed.

"Maybe Noah came up with an idea," she said hopefully. But Noah hadn't mentioned anything last night when they'd talked, and she kind of thought that if he had come up with something he thought would work, he probably would've run it by her. Not that they were great friends or anything, but they had talked about more intimate things last night than she had in a long time. Than she had with almost anyone else she knew. And she had a feeling that Noah had bared a little of his heart to her too.

They walked in and found seats towards the front. Noah was already on the platform, deep in conversation with one of the McBride brothers, maybe Roland, but she wasn't sure.

She did see Pastor Johnson chatting with Marjorie McBride, who was already settled in a chair with a blanket over her lap. The woman looked thin and frail, and Aunt Vivian tsked when she saw her.

Grace didn't know her any other way, and she didn't look any worse than she did the last time Grace had seen her just a few days ago, so she didn't say anything.

"If everyone could find a seat and stop talking, we'll get this started," Noah said, leaning into the microphone and looking over the crowd.

She didn't think it was her imagination that his eyes stopped when they met hers, and the look on his face went from serious and businesslike to a bit of a smile.

Which she returned.

Her heart did some weird twirly thing, and her stomach twisted, but not in a bad way. In a very good, "I see someone I like and maybe I'm a little attracted to" kind of way.

Was she attracted to him? She'd have to think about that. She was just getting used to the idea of thinking of him as her friend. She definitely wasn't used to thinking of him as someone she was attracted to.

"All right everyone, if you can be quiet, we'll get this started. I'm just gonna say up front that I haven't come up with anything. I've called every other band I can think of who could possibly draw as big a crowd as the one that canceled on us. And they're all booked. That's not even to say I have any idea where we would get any money to pay them. I guess I was just going to ask them to do it out of the kindness of their hearts. But I didn't even get that far. Does anyone else have any suggestions?"

"I thought you told me you had an idea," someone shouted from the other side of the room. Grace couldn't see who, and she didn't recognize the voice.

"All right. Wilson is right. I do have an idea, but I can't guarantee it's going to work." He paused. "First, does anyone else have any ideas?"

Jones, the veterinarian who'd offered his lawyer at the last meeting, stood up and looked around.

No one said anything for a full three minutes.

Finally, Jones looked back at Noah.

"Sounds to me like you can go on right ahead with your idea, because I don't hear anyone else coming up with anything."

"Yeah, what are you thinking?" someone else shouted.

"Better than anything I've come up with, which is nothing," someone else said.

"All right. Just hold on. Don't get excited, because this isn't that good." Noah shifted on the platform, and then his eyes searched the crowd again until they found her. It was almost as though he were drawing strength by looking at her. It made her smile, and she nodded at him in a "go ahead, I'm listening" kind of way.

Once she did that, he broke eye contact and looked out over the rest of the crowd.

"All right. Here goes. My thought is that I, along with someone who might possibly be willing to help me, who I'm not going to name because I haven't gotten a full yes from them, might take as many people from the community as we can and create different groups of musicians. I'm already working with an adult group."

Grace remembered the ad she'd seen in the candy cane shop door. She'd forgotten about it.

"Maybe a group of elementary school kids, a group of high school, a group of special needs perhaps, a group of college-age kids. A group of women, a group of men, a group of seniors. We could do handbells, percussion, singing, playing, even dancing. You get the idea. As many as we can. The idea being that the more people we have in the concert actually playing, the more people who will come to see them—see their aunt or their uncle or their grandfather or their little sister come play. It wouldn't be people from all over the country or even the region, but we might be able to get almost every single person in our county out to see someone they know perform. It would be more inclusive, and it would definitely be a community-created concert with everyone involved. It would be less about perfect performance and more about participation and having fun. And I'm sorry, even as I'm saying that it sounds lame, but that's the only thing I could come up with."

"That's a pretty good idea."

"I'd go along with that."

"Sounds like a lot of work, but if you're willing to do it—"

"And I might possibly know someone who would be willing to give a short piano performance afterwards. A big-name person who would draw in a huge crowd. We could—I don't think that person would want to have the entire thing resting on their shoulders, but they would do something along with Noah's idea."

Grace licked her lips, which were suddenly dry. She couldn't believe she had jumped up and started talking. That wasn't like her at all, and especially not after what had happened. And, considering that she was volunteering to get in front of a crowd and perform, she doubly couldn't believe it.

But Noah stared at her, shock and disbelief and excitement dawning on his face, and she couldn't look away from it.

He knew exactly who she was talking about when she said she knew a person who would perform.

And she knew who he meant when he said he might have someone to help him.

Maybe their talk had gone deeper than what she thought, because they seemed to be communicating without words right now.

"That all sounds great to me. It's better than any other ideas I've heard anyone say."

"Nobody's given any other ideas!"

"Exactly!"

"All right then. I'm gonna open the floor for anyone else who has any thoughts or suggestions, or wants to make any comments on our offerings. But, if this stands, this is what we're going to attempt."

He was quiet, and the whole room held its breath and waited.

Finally, after no one said a word, Noah hit the gavel on the podium and said, "All right. Meeting adjourned. We'll do our best."

Grace sat there, trying to figure out exactly how much time they had. From her calculations, they had less than three weeks to pull it all together. Three weeks. Her throat tightened, and her chest constricted. She took a deep breath and tried to blow it out. They could do this. She and Noah, together.

Chapter Sixteen

In all the excitement after the meeting, Grace had not been able to see Noah. People had swarmed the platform, wanting details about everything, including —she assumed—who he was going to be doing it with.

She and Vivian had slipped out, and she thought maybe Noah would stop by on his way home. But he hadn't.

Or maybe he hadn't gone home yet. She wasn't sure.

She set her knitting down and got up.

"Would you like a cup of coffee?" she asked Aunt Vivian who worked on a gingerbread house at the table.

"Why don't you take a cup over to Noah. I'm betting he could use it right now."

Her eyes widened, but she didn't know why she was surprised. Aunt Vivian knew her better than anyone, other than maybe Noah. And that was odd, since she'd only talked to Noah a handful of times in her entire life.

"Is he home?"

"He walked by when you were in the restroom. He peeked in, but I waved, and he kept walking."

"I didn't know."

"You didn't ask. I would've told you."

"Let me go put some coffee on. Or maybe hot chocolate. It's kind of late for coffee."

"I think that's a good idea."

Aunt Vivian dabbed a little icing on a rectangular piece of gingerbread and gently set it in place. It was too early for her to go to bed. And Grace felt a little guilty leaving her. One of the benefits of having a houseguest was to have company in the evening, so she could chat and not be alone.

Grace put milk on to heat and then glanced out the window.

She could see Noah pacing in the music room, running a hand through his hair, stopping, and then pacing more.

Obviously, he was as agitated as she was.

It didn't take long for the milk to warm up. She poured it into steaming cups, added some whipped cream on top, and headed for the door.

When Aunt Vivian saw her coming, she got up to open it for her.

"I'm going to head to bed, but I'll leave the living room light on for you and the door unlocked."

"I won't be long," Grace said, truly believing that.

"I wouldn't be surprised if you might be a little bit longer than you think. You guys have some things to talk about."

Grace knew they did. But, she wasn't sure either one of them was ready to talk. What were they going to say? Their ideas felt like they were half-baked, and now that they were away from the meeting, Grace had no idea why she had stood up and volunteered what she did, on top of what Noah had volunteered. How were they ever going to pull that off?

And were people going to come?

She swallowed against her doubts and fear and walked across the deserted street, heading toward the music store.

Maybe Aunt Vivian had texted him to let him know that she was coming, or maybe he had a sixth sense, because he was at the front door of the music store opening it before she had time to figure out how in the world she was going to knock with two mugs of hot chocolate in her hands.

"Good evening," she said, feeling a little bit dumb. Maybe he didn't drink hot chocolate, and maybe he didn't want to see her.

"I looked for you earlier in your living room, but you weren't there."

"Aunt Vivian said you went by, but I was in the restroom. I didn't realize it, or I would've come over right away. I assume you feel like we need to talk too?"

"Definitely. And, I feel so much calmer whenever you're around."

His hair stuck up because he'd been running his hand through it all evening, and although his face looked just as serious and businesslike as usual, she felt the same comfort and security that she always did in his presence. It was funny that he was now admitting that he felt the same thing with her.

"I wasn't sure if maybe you'd like a drink?" she asked, offering him one of the mugs of hot chocolate.

"That smells like hot chocolate, and it sounds like just the thing."

"It is. Chocolate makes everything better, right?" she asked, lifting a brow and stepping inside as he closed the door behind her.

She honestly wasn't sure what could make this better. She had volunteered to perform, and she wasn't even sure she could.

"I need to apologize for not staying. I did look for you, but also... I suppose I was running away a little bit. I don't know why I volunteered the things I did. Probably because I really wanted to help the town, which has been so nice and friendly and welcoming to me. But, I know that I'm not sure I can do what I said I was going to."

Her words hung in the air as she looked at him, waiting for him to respond.

"Well that makes two of us."

His response was simple, and somehow it made her feel better.

He was going out on a limb as well. And he didn't know whether he would be able to do what he said.

"Let's go sit down. Maybe in the music room?"

"That's fine."

"We could go upstairs and sit in the living room, but we might need the piano if we start brainstorming about things." She nodded and he turned and led the way through the store and into the back where the piano sat.

His eyes crinkled a bit as he indicated two comfortable-looking chairs in the corner of the music room. He waited until she chose one and sat down before he sat down beside her.

"These chairs are for parents or siblings or anyone who might accompany kids to their music lessons. I don't usually use them myself, but they're kind of comfortable." He settled down with a sigh, and she smiled.

Just in the few minutes that she'd been here, he seemed like he'd settled down and was much calmer and less anxious. Maybe what he'd said about her helping to calm him down was actually true.

Not that she didn't believe him, but it was hard to believe that they gave each other the same sense of calm and strength.

"It's kind of you to provide such comfortable chairs for your students' families."

"Sometimes listening to someone practice an instrument and learn can be very difficult. I suppose at the very least I could offer them a comfortable place to sit."

"I know that well."

It was true, she did know how badly an instrument could sound before a person got competent on it. "I've heard violins are one of the worst."

"Honestly, I feel like horns would be terrible. They have a loud, sometimes obnoxious sound when they're not played correctly, and it's true the violins screech, but that's not the kind of noise that you can't get away from. A horn, on the other hand..." He shuddered in an exaggerated way.

They laughed together.

She felt more at ease than she had since she had stood up in the community meeting and volunteered herself.

"I'm sorry I jumped in the middle of your idea at the meeting."

He waved a hand. "No apology necessary. I think our goals are the same. We both love this town and want to help it. And you offered the only thing you knew, and all you had. I admire that. Especially when you're not even sure you can do it. That to me is what bravery is."

She swallowed hard. His words, sincere and serious, made her spine stiffen and her chest feel deeper and bigger. Like maybe she really was brave. Maybe she really could do it. Maybe there really was some kind of character inside of her that made her do things that other people might admire.

"Thank you."

She couldn't think of anything else to say, and those words seemed to cover it all.

She took a sip of her hot chocolate, enjoying the aroma and the comfortable silence as she sifted through her mind, trying to figure out what they needed to talk about. It seemed like everything. There was so much, she didn't know where to begin.

"So, is it okay if I expound on my idea?"

"I'd like to hear it. Also, I assume you meant that you thought I might help you. You'd asked, and I told you I would think about it. I've thought about it."

"And?"

"My answer is yes. I'll do whatever I need to. Even though I'm not sure I'll be any good at it, and I have to admit I'm scared."

That made his lips turn up.

"Sometimes we need to do it afraid."

"Yeah. I'm learning that. And to let go of my ideas of perfectionism and just realize that I'll prepare as much as I can, and then allow the chips to fall where they will."

"And pray. We can do a lot of praying between now and then."

"I don't know. It's only three weeks."

"True. I'm trying not to think of the time limitations. But I suppose I should." He seemed to hesitate, then he said, a little softer, "I wouldn't have volunteered if I didn't think you were going to say yes. I can't imagine doing this without you."

She nodded and took another sip of her hot chocolate, not knowing what to say. She was honored. Flattered. And, something warm had started to curl in her stomach. Something that made her feel like maybe she wasn't the only one who felt... attraction? Was that what it was? She thought maybe, but she wasn't sure.

"All right. This is what I was thinking." He began, and then he outlined in a little more detail what he had talked about during the meeting. She listened with rapt attention, picturing his vision in her head and seeing how that could work. Especially combined with what she had suggested.

"So, there will be at least five mini concerts. We won't be able to teach them a whole pile of songs in three weeks, but everyone could learn at least one, whether it's singing or bells or instruments."

"And then we'll end with a mini concert of me."

"Exactly." He had long ago set his hot chocolate aside, and now he leaned forward with his arms resting on his knees. "We'll bring in the locals because of all the people who are playing in the small groups. And then we'll bring in non-locals to hear you."

"And you."

"My name isn't gonna bring anyone in. It's going to be you."

"Maybe people will hear you and you'll get offers."

He shook his head. "I'm not sure I want that. Honestly. Once upon a time I did. I had to give up my Juilliard offer, and that was really hard. But my family came first. Now that they're gone, I could travel all over the place, but I'm not interested in that anymore. Not really."

He seemed like he was thinking about something else, but he didn't say.

"This could be a really amazing thing, but I can't do it by myself."

"And I can't either. But I've already told you I'm scared, and I'm not sure I can."

"I'm confident God will give us everything we need."

"I wish I had that confidence. But I'll trust you, and I definitely trust Him. Just go slow, okay?"

He reached out and took her hand and squeezed it.

He let go immediately. It was just a simple gesture, one of solidarity and friendship. But, long after she left, and long after she had gone to bed well after midnight, she thought about it. Thought about working with Noah, his confidence and his ability to get things done. His protectiveness and his willingness to give up himself in order to be a blessing to others.

Those were things she had always admired, and she'd never found them in such a concentrated way in a man.

She snuggled under the covers and held her hand close.

She didn't know where this was going to go, but she did know that she would enjoy every second of working with Noah Connor.

Chapter Seventeen

"Thanks for fixing us up with a room, Kate," Noah said.

"Of course. It's for the community. And the school is paid for with taxes from the folks who live here. It's really everyone's building."

Kate smiled and then waved as she hurried away to the meeting she needed to attend after school, leaving Noah in the room by himself.

Grace would be there any moment. They'd been texting back and forth, and Noah had let her know that he had secured a room with Kate Henderson for them to practice in, since the lesson room behind the shop wasn't nearly big enough.

They still had sign-up sheets out all over town for the groups they were putting together, but the elementary and high school music groups had already been practicing with the teacher who left. It was just a matter of them taking over where the music teacher had left off.

"I'm sorry I'm a little late. You know Aunt Vivian is watching your store while you're gone and she had asked me to switch the laundry and check the crockpot, and I was almost here before I remembered that I had forgotten to do that."

Grace arrived, breathless, unwrapping a scarf from around her neck, her cheeks a becoming shade of pink and her eyes sparkling. That crazy purple hat brought out the blue in them, and he was tempted to take it off, to touch her hair.

He shook that feeling off and smiled instead.

"You're plenty early. The kids shouldn't be arriving for another fifteen minutes or so."

"I know. But I wanted to be here to help you set up. This is supposed to be both of us working together, not just you."

"You bring more to the table than I do, so it's only right that I do more behind the scenes."

She waved a hand in the air, like her name recognition really didn't matter, when they both knew it did. They would not have been able to do this without it. Of course, she probably wouldn't have had the courage to volunteer without him beside her.

So maybe they just needed each other. He liked that. The two of them facing the world together.

They spent the next fifteen minutes arranging chairs in a circle, talking about the best ways to place them, how they would lead off, and what they hoped to convey and accomplish.

He felt like they were ready when the first student arrived.

Grace was excellent at putting them at ease and chatting with them naturally. He wanted to stand back and just admire her. Because she did it all so well.

Soon all the students were there and had their instruments out and had been seated.

He went to the front and directed everyone's attention to himself.

"I know you've already practiced the music, and I've looked over it. It looks like some really fun stuff. Does anyone have any favorites?"

They couldn't play all the pieces, but he didn't want to cut any pieces that any of the children had their hearts set on performing. That's what he tried to weed out in the next few minutes, with Grace helping him keep track of who liked what songs.

By the end of his questions, Grace was able to come up to him and show him a list of the songs they could take out.

"All right. We're going to be performing on December 23rd, outside in the town square. It's going to be cold, so we don't want to play too long, because we don't want our fingers to fall off."

There was laughter from all of the children, and Grace's eyes twinkled. He would make corny jokes all day if it would get her to smile. "So, I have a list of four songs that it seems like no one's going to be super upset if we cut. I'm gonna read them out loud, and you guys can let me know if it's going to bother you if we don't end up doing all of them."

He named the titles of the songs while Grace carefully watched to see if there was any reaction from the children. When they learned that one of the songs was going to be dropped, some of them actually cheered.

Sometimes, as a musician, you had to play music that you didn't like. In fact, there were multiple times that he had to play music that he didn't care for. But most of the time he loved what he did, but he knew he did a better job when he enjoyed the music he had. Since these children were not professionals, and not adults, and since they had to pare down the amount of songs they could perform, it only made sense to keep the ones they enjoyed.

Learning to do things one didn't like was a process that happened over years and years, and if the children continued to take lessons, they would have to learn that lesson along with everything else. But it wasn't one they had to learn this Christmas.

Chapter Eighteen

race lost herself in the enjoyment of teaching, the excitement on the children's faces, and working with someone who had her back constantly.

In the cutthroat world of professional musicians, sure, she had friends, but she had never had anyone who had her back the way Noah did. He wasn't out to one-up her, or take her chair, her position, or to try to play better than she did or schmooze up to someone better than she did, but was behind her, trying to make sure that she was successful, as she was doing with him. Plus, working with children was far less pressure than working with a professional group. They had fun, they enjoyed it, they laughed and their eyes sparkled. This was what music was supposed to do to people. Not make them so anxious that they ended up having panic attacks and couldn't play at all.

When had she lost the joy of performing, of playing just for the sake of playing? Of performing just because she loved it?

As Noah got the children started, and they got their music out and played their first notes, it didn't sound great. But the kids were having a good time, so was she, and Noah seemed to be enjoying everything as well.

About forty-five minutes into the practice, which they had agreed would only last an hour and no longer, Mason came to the door. She knew Mason from the medical center where he worked after school.

None of the children noticed, because they were in the middle of playing an arrangement of "Silent Night," and she casually walked to the door without drawing attention to him.

"Noah is a natural with these kids. I've heard them practice before, and they sounded terrible." Mason shuddered in mock horror.

She laughed and pitched her voice low.

"When you're first starting out learning an instrument, horrible is probably what you should expect."

"Well you should've seen the other teacher trying to work with the kids. They got angry and frustrated and slammed books around and insulted the kids, and they were nothing like Noah. I've been listening cause I've been working in the office across the hall for some extra credit to make up grades, and I've been listening. Noah is amazing with kids. I just thought I'd pop in and give him a thumbs-up. But I don't want to bother anyone."

"I'll tell him what you said. And I know he'll appreciate it. He's bitten off a pretty big chunk, and he's not sure he can chew it."

"But he's got you to help him. What more could a guy want?" He grinned and then ducked back out before Grace could ask him what in the world he meant.

As they came to a particularly hard part of the passage, Noah stopped and motioned to her to give him a hand. She went up, and they helped some of the children individually with that spot. As she did, she thought to herself that teaching was performing without performance anxiety. She was helping others to perform, and they were taking what she was giving them and using it for themselves and their performance. They would take a little bit of her with them wherever they went. She loved that idea. Loved that she was pouring into a child and that what she gave would last for the rest of that child's life, possibly making them a better person, and definitely a better musician if they took her advice and utilized it.

She was still thinking about that after the kids had left and they were cleaning up the room. They wanted to leave it spotless since the school had been gracious enough to allow them to use it without giving them a difficult time.

"I thought that went really well," Noah said as he closed the door after the last student left.

"Far better than I thought it was going to. The kids were such a joy to work with. They love what they do."

"I think anymore you almost have to love the idea of music or playing it yourself or something, because so few people actually put the work into learning an instrument."

"You could be right. Or maybe the love of music is fostered at home somehow?"

"It could be. I know my parents were instrumental—no pun intended—in my love of music. All of my siblings have it. Some of my favorite times with my family were when we all sat around together and sang in the evenings. What a great time as a family."

"That sounds really nice," Grace said, thinking about her own childhood and how it was nothing like that unless the extended family got together. Definitely not on a regular evening.

"How would you like to go out for hot chocolate? As a celebration for how well things went today. I don't know if the rest of the groups will be this easy, but I'm excited about it now, when before I was... doing it mostly for duty and dreading it a good bit."

Grace laughed. She knew exactly what he meant.

"Hot chocolate sounds amazing."

Whether he was asking her out to celebrate or just because he wanted to go, she didn't care. She wanted to spend more time with Noah.

It didn't take long to finish cleaning up the room, and they decided to walk to the diner. It wasn't far. Plus, it was a warm, sunny day, which matched both of their moods. They chatted easily about the practice session, what they thought went well, a few things they thought they could improve, and strategy for younger children and older children, along with adults and special needs. That was the group Grace was really looking forward to. They would be especially enthusiastic, she suspected, and probably the most fun to work with.

Not that she wanted to play favorites or anything.

"I'm glad it went so well," she said as they sat down across from each other at the diner. Their conversation had flowed so easily, and while they hadn't talked about anything deep, their silences had been easy with no expectations. She felt completely at ease with Noah. More than she had with anyone else in her entire life, including her parents.

"Did your family sing together when you were a child? I said that earlier, and you kind of got quiet. I wanted to ask you about it, but... I didn't want to ruin the good mood."

"Oh, I don't know that you'd be ruining a good mood," she said.

The waitress came to take their drink orders, and they both ordered hot chocolate with extra whipped cream. Then, after she walked away, Grace continued.

"My parents were very strict. They were demanding and perfectionistic. They were both very wealthy, very successful in their fields, and I know that the way they raised me came from an attitude of them wanting me to be successful too, you know?"

"It's good that you can see that. I think a lot of people can't." Noah sighed and moved his placemat around a bit. "I think they just see their parents as being mean and unkind, but there are very few people whose parents actually did not like them. There are a lot of people whose parents made mistakes. Mine included. And I made a lot of mistakes raising my siblings, but that gave me a different perspective. I see that my parents weren't being mean. They were trying to raise me to be a better person. They were trying to show me the way."

"Exactly. I figured that out. I didn't have any siblings to raise. But I wish I had more affection from my parents. I wish that they would have not forced me to practice for hours and hours and hours on end. I wish I could've gone out and played with my friends, or watched TV sometimes, or just hung out and sung for the fun of it like you described. But everything was always so serious. I had to practice, I had to make the audition, I had to be first chair. I had to get the part. Get the A. And again, I know they loved me. And they were doing that out of love. But yes, there was a while when I resented it. Still, when the extended family got together, we sang and played and I loved it. That most often happened at Aunt Vivian's house. Which is why it has such special memories. I just wish more of my childhood was like that, and that I didn't resent what my parents did."

"Of course. Your childhood is gone, and it was a pretty tough one. But, let me ask you a question."

"Okay." She was curious. What in the world could he possibly want to know?

"Do you think you would be a successful musician today if your parents had not been so demanding?"

"That's easy. No. Absolutely not. I thought you were going to ask me a hard question."

"I think that there are some people who would have to think about that for a while and might not give their parents the credit they deserve. But it's obvious to me that, while your childhood maybe wasn't ideal, you appreciate it anyway."

"I think sometimes we don't appreciate the hard things."

"I agree. Like my parents dying. I didn't appreciate that for a really long time. I thought God was being mean. Honestly, I was tempted to walk away from my faith. The only reason I didn't was because I knew I had my siblings coming after me, and while I was angry at God and wanted to walk away from Him out of spite, I didn't want my siblings to not have a relationship with Him." He shook his head, a little grin tugging up his mouth. "That just shows how immature I was. Right? Because obviously, I knew there was a

God, and I knew that He was right about everything, but I just didn't want to give Him credit because I was angry about losing my parents."

"I'm not saying you were right, but that's a totally justifiable feeling. I don't think that there are too many people who wouldn't have felt that way."

"I don't know. Some people seem to be able to go through hardships and handle it so much better than I do. But I doubted myself. I didn't think I was good enough. I didn't know how in the world I could raise my siblings, because I was such a mess."

"You don't seem like a mess. I'd be curious to know what your siblings think about that."

"Oh I think they would say that I was a mess most of the time." He said that immediately, and then at her raised brow, he tilted his head. "Maybe not. Maybe they would say that they appreciated what I did. I know that several of them have said that they were glad they weren't the oldest and didn't have that responsibility dumped on their shoulders."

"Did it ever occur to you that maybe they left the house in a hurry because they felt like you had done enough? That they were trying to relieve you of your burden?"

Noah seemed to think about that, because he was still for a while.

Grace spoke again, feeling it out, because she hadn't really thought about it.

"I'm just wondering if that's their way of releasing you from the responsibilities that you took on. I mean, have you ever told them that you would prefer that they come back? I mean, I assume they all know that they're welcome back anytime."

"Absolutely. They are welcome back anytime, but you're right. I'm not sure I let them know. Maybe they are thinking they're doing me a favor by not coming."

"That reminds me, Aunt Vivian said that you're welcome to come to our house for Christmas if you want to. I didn't know if you would or not, though." Grace bit her lip. Aunt Vivian had asked her to say something to Noah, and she had hesitated, because she didn't want to come off as being too forward, and she also didn't want him to feel like he had to if he had somewhere else he'd rather go. Or maybe he was the kind of person who would rather spend it alone.

"I don't want to put you guys out."

"You wouldn't be. Vivian would love the company. I didn't realize until I came, but I think she was lonely."

"That makes sense. I understand that better now that the last of my siblings has moved out. Honestly, when my youngest sister went to college, it was almost a relief to have a little bit of time to myself, you know?"

"I can imagine. But I've always been alone. So I don't understand as well as I should."

"Yeah, well it's just having the responsibility all the time. When she left, I still wanted to keep up with her, but it was her life now. And I had time to sit down in the evening and play the piano instead of eating supper if I wanted to. And I could stay up until midnight or 3 o'clock in the morning if I felt like it. Of course, I'm getting older and I don't really feel like it." He laughed.

She chuckled along with him. "I know exactly what you mean. It used to be that I could practice for hours and hours and hours, and it would be five o'clock in the morning and I wouldn't even realize it. But now, about eleven o'clock I start to think that it's time for bed."

"I feel like I'm older than you are, because I think I feel that even earlier at times." His voice trailed off, but he didn't say anything more and she left it at that.

"I never thought that a music store would be able to survive in a small town. I don't want to pry, but... Is it hard?" She was curious, but she didn't know how to ask what she wanted to know without sounding like she was putting her nose in his business.

"Not gonna lie. It is. Although, now that I just have me, I don't feel quite the pressure that I used to. But... For example, right now the roof is leaking and my furnace is about to give out, if the clang and bang it makes every time it starts and stops is any indication."

"Could you have it serviced?"

"The last time I did, the service guy said he had done everything he could for it. He said the next time I wanted my furnace serviced I should call an undertaker. That was an exact quote."

She laughed. At least he had a sense of humor about it.

"It's not all doom and gloom. Usually, I have an emergency fund, but one of my siblings ran into someone who needed some help, and I guess I just didn't even think twice. I wrote a check out and there went that."

"They're like your children."

"I suppose in a way. He's gonna pay me back, and hopefully that will happen before my roof and furnace give out."

Her eyes narrowed a bit. "You know, I thought this was such a great town. And I've heard about the Secret Saint that goes around helping people?" She paused, waiting for him to nod before she continued. "But... You'd think that the Secret Saint would want to help you. I mean, not that other people don't deserve it just as much, but isn't that what he's for? I guess it just makes me doubt everything I was thinking."

"I didn't mean to make you get down on the town. And the Secret Saint is... It's a really great addition to our town. But, he can't help everyone." Noah's words were slow and measured as though he were thinking about each one before they came out.

She supposed he didn't want to say anything bad about his town, even though she knew she was right. The Secret Saint definitely should be helping one of the pillar members of the community, otherwise, what was the point?

"Well, it's a blight on your community." She said the words lightly, almost as though she were joking, but in her heart, she was serious. Any town that would allow someone like Noah to struggle while helping people who contributed less to society didn't deserve to be on a pedestal. It wasn't that it wasn't okay, because it was. They could help whoever they wanted to help. But they didn't deserve special recognition if they didn't either help everyone, or—how did they decide who to help? And who was she to make judgments about who should and shouldn't be helped?

"I think that's something I need to try to get over. Maybe because you've been so kind to me and have really made me love this small town, I feel like you should be on the list of people who definitely get help."

"I guess I see where you're coming from, but I would rather be the kind of person who helps people than the kind of person who needs help. It's not really the place I want to be, you know?"

"I suppose."

She thought about the emails that she had been getting asking if she would perform or teach or speak at various functions and groups. For pay, of course. She had enough money saved up that she didn't need to work for years, or ever again if she handled her money right. But, she could make some extra money. She didn't really have a whole lot of money that she could use, since it was all in investments, but... She could earn money to help him.

"How much do you think the repairs would cost?"

"I haven't priced it out. I guess I'm a little afraid to. Like if I price it out, everything's going to go kaput. But... I suppose four to five thousand." He grinned. "Don't worry about it. God will provide. He always does. Sometimes I feel pressure, but most of the time I've learned to trust Him. He always comes through."

"I admire your faith." She paused for a moment, realizing she was surprised that the waitress had brought their hot chocolate and she hadn't even noticed. Still, it was too hot to drink, so she just let it sit.

"Maybe part of what I'm going through, my stage fright, is a lack of faith in God. Me wanting to control the narrative and what happens. Instead of giving control to God."

"I would agree with that. I feel like life is so much about us preparing, and in your case, practicing, as hard as we can. Doing everything that we can. Because God isn't going to just drop stuff in our lap. He does want us to work. But He wants us to leave it all up to Him too."

"I don't understand that. Like we're just supposed to let God do everything, but we're supposed to do everything too. It doesn't make any sense to me." She shook her head and lifted a hand up. She just couldn't see how that worked. Maybe it was just one of those paradoxes.

"I heard it explained like this once. They weren't talking about this specific thing. I think they were talking more about grace and redemption. But it applies to this as well."

"Okay."

"It's like this. A farmer goes out and he plows the field and he plants a seed and he sprays and he weeds and he makes sure that the soil is the right pH and has all the right nutrients in it and he harvests it and he works hard. He does a lot of work. All the while, he knows that if God does not send the rain, if God does not send the sun, without the oxygen in the air—he can't grow crops. It is not all on him, because without God, the crops can't grow. But, if the farmer doesn't put the work in, the crops also won't grow. But it's out of the farmer's hands. Does that make sense?" He lifted his hands and absently stirred his hot chocolate. The cream on the top wiggled as the chocolate underneath moved.

"I think I see. It's all God, but it's all us too."

"Yes. Exactly. God's not gonna do our work for us. There's work that we have to do that He will not do, but without Him providing what is represented by the sunshine and the rain in that analogy, our work is no good. So, we have to be ready. We have to put the work in, the practice in, the time in, and be ready so that when the rain or the sun or whatever that is in our lives comes, we're ready to do whatever God wants us to do."

"I see."

"And I think that's the way it is with sanctification too. God does all the work for sanctification, but if we are still living in sin and don't care about cleaning up our act, then that work won't take place. Just like if the farmer doesn't plant the seed, no matter how much rain God sends, it can't grow. So yes, we get saved and God comes in and He changes us and it's all God. But we also have decisions to make. Are we going to give up our sin? Are we going to stop doing the things that we know we shouldn't do? Taking the Lord's name in vain. Committing whatever kind of sexual sin. Wasting our time frivolously instead of looking around to see what we can do for the Lord. Reading frivolous books instead of studying our Bibles. Sometimes it's as much a matter of putting things into our life as it is of taking them out."

"That's the truth. I did go through a really long time, years, where I barely opened my Bible. There was so much dust on it, and I put it away somewhere and I forgot where I put it."

"I think we all have times like that in our lives, or we're still reading our Bible, but it's just not doing anything for us, because our focus and our desires are elsewhere."

"But I suppose reading the Bible is one of the most important things, because it will convict us of our sin. Convict us that we're not being kind to people, or we're not treating others the way we should, or we're not giving our lives to the Lord, but instead we're listening to the world and we're putting ourselves first, even though it sounds like a good thing. You know, taking care of ourselves."

That really resonated with Grace, because she had been told to take time off, to heal herself, and while she didn't see anything wrong with that, just the few hours that she spent a day helping others had done more to help her mind get clear than all the time she'd taken for herself. And the Bible clearly said that we were to put others first. If she did that, maybe she wouldn't have so many mental health issues, with everyone sitting around ruminating on themselves.

It was just a theory she had, one that wasn't completely fleshed out, but one that she saw be true in her own life.

Noah picked up his mug and took a sip of his hot chocolate. Grace had to laugh as he pulled his mug away, since there was a bit of whipped topping stuck to his nose. He grinned but made no move to wipe it off.

In a move uncharacteristic for her, she felt her hand come up, and she took one finger and swiped it across his nose. She didn't linger, but maybe she went slightly slower than she needed to.

The air between them felt charged with something, though she wasn't sure what. Noah still smiled, but there were emotions swirling in his eyes she couldn't read.

She had no idea what she looked like, but her heart hammered, and her breathing felt wobbly.

They sat there, staring at each other for what felt like a very long time before Noah finally said, "Thanks."

She grinned and replied, "You're welcome."

She was the first to pull her eyes away, and they dropped to her hot chocolate, which she'd totally forgotten about. She used a spoon to stir it and took a small sip while whatever seemed to be in the air between them relaxed just a bit. Noah cleared his throat.

"I know we were talking about a lot of deep things. Things I don't typically talk to people about."

"Me either. Not without predetermining that we would. I'm sorry. I didn't mean to drag you into anything."

"No, I enjoy conversations like that. I've really been having a good time. But I didn't want you to feel any pressure."

"To perform?" she asked, strangely calm.

"Yes. I know we've been talking about God doing it, and all we have to do is prepare, but that wasn't directed at you in any way. I was just realizing that maybe you felt like it was."

"No. I took it for what it was, just us talking about God, and I actually found it encouraging. Because you're right. Part of my fear, part of what is wrong with me is the fact that I put all this pressure on myself to be good. When in reality, my preparation is what I have control over. God has control over the final product. Maybe it benefits Him more for me to not do well. I mean, that sounds a little bit weird, but it's true."

"Sometimes people can relate more to folks who seem like they're not perfect."

"Yes, exactly. I think the first time you and I talked, it was you sharing with me some of your insecurities, which made me feel like I was a little bit more normal than I felt."

"Is that what it did? I just didn't want you to think that I looked down on you or thought there was something terribly wrong with you for struggling. Because we all struggle."

"Yeah. And maybe that's what the people around me need to see. That I struggle. And that I'm not perfect. And... It's a pride thing where I want to put on this great front where all anyone ever sees is just me being perfect. And I put all of that pressure on myself, and I finally collapsed underneath it."

"Because humans aren't built to take that kind of pressure. We're built to give it to God."

"Exactly. I don't know how to recover from the crash, but I do see that that's the issue. It was me. My pride, wanting to be perfect, the pressure that I placed upon myself, and fear that I wouldn't measure up to the standards that I had for myself. Not standards that anyone else had for me."

"Although, I understand that there probably are people who are looking at you and just waiting for you to fail so they can gloat. Everyone has people around them like that. Unfortunately, that's the way the world is right now."

"And I suppose it's a good thing, because that shows me that that's not the kind of person that I want to be. And it's more important that I be like Jesus than I be perfect. Because if I were perfect, then I wouldn't understand people who weren't. Does that make sense?"

"I think that's exactly right. There are a lot of reasons why God wouldn't want us to be perfect. But I think it's obvious that He doesn't, because the only perfect person in the Bible is Jesus. And even though He was sinless, He still had times where He cried out to God, asking to have God take a trial away from Him. He was so anxious He sweat great drops of blood. It shows that's a very normal human thing, and not necessarily sin."

Even though Grace knew that, it was good to hear someone else say it. To let her know that even Jesus was nervous, anxious, and wished to avoid what He knew lay in His future.

"You guys are just so cute together. I've had six different customers come up and tell me how good you guys look, and I just couldn't stop myself from coming over here and letting you all know." Bree, their waitress, set the check upside down on the table and gushed a little. "You guys need to be careful, because people already have wedding bells ringing in your future." She laughed. "You can take care of that at the cash register or just leave the money on the table. Up to you. Have a great day."

"You too," Noah said.

Grace was too busy blinking. Wedding bells? They looked cute together?

"That's just small towns. Don't let it bother you," Noah said, his voice sounding relaxed. He had already taken the check and looked at it. "If you don't mind, I'll just leave enough money for the bill and the tip right here on the table."

"Oh, I don't—"

"I'm the one who suggested this. I'm gonna pay for it."

He interrupted her, and his voice had a tone that allowed no argument.

"Well then thank you. It was very nice. The conversation, the hot chocolate, and the whole afternoon. I feel like we are on the right track."

"I do too. And hopefully all the buzzing that's been going on with my phone are people who have been messaging me letting me know that they or one of their kids are going to be playing in one of the other groups that we're starting."

"Oh! Can you look really quick?" she asked. They had already stood up, but his words made her excited. Maybe she already felt like they were going to be able to do it. But they needed the people. If he was correct and he had a bunch of people signing up, that was just one more step in the right direction.

"Don't mind at all." He pulled his phone out of his pocket and swiped a bit.

Scrolling up, he seemed to be counting and then he said, "I think we have 10 people for the adults and too many to count for the kids. If... If you don't mind coming over later, we can go over it together. But I better get back to the store. I have a text here from your Aunt Vivian that says that it's starting to feel cool in the building and the heat doesn't seem to be kicking on."

Her stomach sank. "You called it."

"Don't look so worried. God'll work something out."

"Are you for real? You really don't have money to buy a furnace, do you?"

"I do not."

"And you're just gonna be calm about this?"

"Yeah. I guess if people come in the store and it's cold, they can hurry up and buy something, right?" He laughed a little and then set money and the check on the table before allowing her to walk before him to the door, which he opened for her.

She couldn't believe it. He was so calm. So totally chill.

Well, she had a few messages of her own, and maybe she could answer one.

"I know you said five thousand dollars together. And I don't mean to pry, but how much do you think the furnace would be?"

"Probably a little under half that. But honestly, I'm not sure. I haven't priced furnaces out for a long time. They might've gone drastically up in price."

"I see."

She thought about a couple of the offers that she had been determined to dismiss out of hand. She didn't want to do anything big, but she could do something small.

Yeah, she smiled to herself as she thought about it.

"So... I don't mean to invite myself over, but it doesn't seem fair that you're constantly coming over to my house."

"It sounds like we might freeze over at yours. Why don't you come over to mine this evening. Aunt Vivian might be there, so if that bothers you?"

"It does not. Not in the slightest. She's a sweet lady, and I appreciate her holding down the fort. Afternoons are usually pretty slow, but it's great to have someone with a little bit of musical background that I can depend on."

"She's enjoying it. She told me how she enjoys getting out. She wouldn't want to do it on a regular basis or have that kind of expectation placed on her, but to do it once in a while makes her happy."

"Good to know."

"All right then," he said as they came to a stop in front of her aunt's house. "I'll see you this evening."

"Why don't you come in time for supper? I put some things in the crockpot, and they'll be ready shortly before you close for the day."

"I might close early if it's that cold."

"All right. Then we'll expect you for supper."

"Sounds good."

They stood, looked at each other for just a moment, and neither one of them really wanted to walk away. Grace knew she didn't for sure. She wanted to stay with Noah, with his calm, protective presence that made her feel cared for and safe. She supposed that was something that as a woman, especially, she really wanted. To feel safe.

He was the one to move first, and he lifted a hand, smiled, and then turned around.

She wanted to watch him walk away, but turned and walked toward the door. It was unlocked, and she walked right in, looking back in time to see that he looked back to make sure that she got in okay.

She smiled and lifted a hand and waved. She liked that. Checking on her. It made her feel cared for.

Chapter Nineteen

Noah felt like whistling as he walked back to the shop after leaving Grace. The afternoon had been a smashing success in his book. Not just the fact that practice had gone really, really well with the kids, but more so the fact that he had gotten to spend the entire afternoon with Grace. And she was everything he thought she was, and so much more. She had deep thoughts and had really thought about what God was and how she could best serve Him. She was willing to make changes in her life to be more aligned with God's purpose and plan. She was great with kids, and she even seemed to be a little bit on his side, almost against the town.

He felt kind of bad about that though. He wanted to tell her that the Secret Saint could hardly fix his furnace, since he was the Secret Saint.

He had been so tempted to tell her that. So tempted. He had also been tempted to let her know that part of the reason he didn't have any money to fix the furnace was not just because he had given his emergency fund to his sibling to help out someone in need, but also because he had been spending every extra cent he had on getting things for the Secret Saint to help other people. So much of what they did was donated, but he would buy groceries, blankets, and gifts out of his own pocket. He didn't mind at all and felt like he would rather spend his money on that than anything else in the world. And now that none of his siblings were home, he could. He didn't have to worry about any additional expenses. He could eat as cheaply as possible and give all of his money away. Of course he wanted to be a good steward of what he had and be able to take care of emergencies that cropped up, and he thought he had that covered. Obviously, he was wrong about that. But, he wouldn't have it any other way. What groceries was he not going to buy so he could save money to cover his furnace? What blankets was he not going to buy? What electric bill was he not going to pay for someone else?

Yeah. It was what it was.

He thanked Aunt Vivian and informed her that he was coming to her house for supper. She laughed and said that Grace had already told her, and she was looking forward to it. She told him to bring his appetite.

He laughed as she walked out, but indeed, she was right. It was freezing in the room. But, years ago, almost twenty, if he recalled correctly, the furnace had gone out when his parents were still alive, and he remembered for a few days his dad had a space heater and used that to heat the shop. It would work again, although it was not good for the instruments to have great fluctuations in temperature, and it really wasn't good for them to have dry air, but it would have to do for now. He would call the local HVAC company either later that afternoon or first thing in the morning. He had a few things he needed to catch up on and he had students coming for lessons, and he needed to get the store warmed up first.

It didn't take long for him to dig through the closet and find the space heaters his dad had used. The register was open to the downstairs from upstairs, and he knew the heat would go up and warm the upstairs too. He would just have to make sure no one burned themselves on it, but otherwise, he could use it for the rest of the winter if he really had to.

Lord, I don't know where you're gonna provide the funds from, but I gave away what I had, trusting that you would provide. And I'm expecting you to do that. Or else allow me to figure out a way to work around it. This is in your hands.

By the time his first student arrived, he had the space heaters plugged in, one in his store and one in the back in the lesson room. It was still a little chilly, but not as bad as it had been.

Normally, he enjoyed giving lessons, but he watched the clock a lot more than he typically did, because, he had to face it, he was looking forward to seeing Grace again. There was just something about her, and he felt drawn to her, plus he enjoyed her company. They laughed together and had fun. At least he did. He'd love to know what she thought. He supposed he could ask her, but she might feel like she needed to be polite when she really preferred not to be around him as much as he wanted to be around her.

He gave himself a hard time for being a coward. He should just ask her out. Why not? What did he have to lose?

He supposed their working relationship. They were going to be working together for the next three weeks, and if she didn't want to go out with him, that could make everything awkward. Or, it could plant a seed in her head that he was definitely interested, and maybe she would think about it and decide that she was too.

He found himself with a silly grin on his face and was thankful that his student was looking at the music and playing and not paying attention to his teacher being all sappy over a girl.

He had watched each of his siblings go through various stages of romantic interest, and he'd always found it funny. And now, look at him. Getting all sappy and smiley just thinking about Grace.

He was so looking forward to it that he barely noticed everything was pretty warm by the time he flipped the "closed" sign over and walked out. Yeah, he was closing a little early, but he could let everyone know it was because of the heat.

Maybe that would be a good thing. Maybe some of the donors who usually donated for the Secret Saint things would get together, pool their resources, and be able to spring for a furnace for him.

Except he didn't want that. He didn't want people who might be donating to someone else to give their money to him. He would rather see other needy people get it.

Was he needy?

He didn't want to think of himself that way, but the flipside was, he loved giving to people, loved doing things for people, and got a lot of satisfaction out of that. Why shouldn't he be one of the ones who needed things given to him at some point? That way he could let someone else have the good feeling of doing something kind and generous for someone else.

He hadn't fleshed that thought out very well before he arrived at Vivian's Victorian house and knocked on the door.

Grace answered, opening the door wide, her cheeks flushed, her hair pulled straight back from her head and held in a ponytail which fell down between her shoulder blades, shining and catching the light as she moved.

He could admire her hair all day long.

"You made it!" she said, looking very pleased to see him, and not at all like she was tired of his company, even though they had spent almost the entire afternoon together.

"Wouldn't miss it," he said.

"Was it your furnace? Was it unfixable?"

"It was the furnace. Yes. And I didn't get to call anyone about it. By the time I dug out the space heaters, my first student was there, so I needed to give a lesson, and once I was done with my lessons for the day, it was time to come here."

"Oh I'm sorry. Maybe inviting you to come here made it so you couldn't call about your furnace." He stepped in, and she closed the door behind him, her brows drawing down, concern on her face.

"No. I'll call first thing in the morning. Frank's pretty good. I mean, he did tell me that I was going to need an undertaker the next time for my furnace rather than having it serviced, but... He'll be fair with me." Maybe he'd even have payment plans. But he wasn't going to worry about that now. He would worry about that tomorrow and take care of it then. "In the meantime, the space heaters are doing their job, but my house doesn't smell nearly as good as yours does."

"It does smell good, doesn't it?" She grinned. "We have slow cooker fajita soup in the crockpot, and I have been dying for the last twenty minutes ever since Aunt Vivian took the lid off. It smells so good. She even made bread for it."

"Homemade bread? I am so in," he said, rubbing his hands together.

If it was possible, she smiled even bigger, and he found himself getting stuck watching it. What would it be like to sit across from that smile every day? He could only imagine it would be wonderful. Interesting that he'd never considered wanting to sit across from anyone's smile for the rest of his life.

Maybe he'd been too busy with his siblings, or maybe he just hadn't met Grace.

"Come in," Aunt Vivian said from the doorway of the kitchen. "Don't just stand there. The poor man is probably hungry, Grace. We've gotta feed him." She waited until they started moving before she looked at Grace. "That's something you need to know about men. They're always hungry."

They all laughed together. He helped get ready for the meal, and then they all sat down together.

They asked him to say grace, which he was more than happy to do. Yeah, his furnace needed to be replaced, and his roof was still leaking, but he felt like he'd been very blessed. Maybe it was just the good company, good friends, the security of being in a town where he knew that people would take care of him if he really needed it. But also the knowledge that God would provide. He was more secure and sure about that than ever.

He said to Aunt Vivian, "I hope you don't mind if Grace and I talk a little shop."

"Not at all. She told me that was what you were planning on

doing. And I'm curious. I hope you don't mind if I eavesdrop while you guys talk shop."

"I don't," he said, lifting his brows at Grace.

"I would probably tell her what we said anyway."

He laughed a little at that and shrugged his shoulders. He didn't care who she told.

"Well I just wanted to let you know that we were talking about all of the people who had texted me when we left the diner, and we have enough adults to have a group and enough high school students to have a group. Actually we could probably do a boys' group and a girls' group if we would like or a singing group and a bells group. Whatever. And, we have eight special needs kids who would love to participate."

"Those were the ones I was the most excited about. I know that that is a little bit crazy, but they're always so enthusiastic and happy, and I think working with them will be super fun."

"They'll be a real crowd pleaser if we pick the right music," Noah said, already having several pieces in mind.

"I'll leave that up to you. I'm sure you know better than I do, but I'm definitely looking forward to that, and that's great news!"

"Yeah. I almost blurted it out as soon as I walked in the door, but I thought I probably ought to do all the social niceties first."

"We don't stand on tradition too much here," Aunt Vivian said. "If you want to burst out with news, go ahead and do it. I can't guarantee that we won't at some point either."

Grace shared a look with her aunt, and it was easy to see the affection between the two of them.

"I was hoping to start tomorrow afternoon. I know you said every afternoon was free—"

"I'm sorry. I had an appointment come up tomorrow. But everything else this week is free. I could do it tomorrow afternoon, but I can't stay late."

He blinked. What had come up so quickly? Surely she wasn't sick?

"I'm sorry. It was on my calendar, and I just kind of forgot about it. It's nothing important." She shook her head a little and smiled at him, and it was the smile that did it. Whatever it was, he believed her that it wasn't important.

He nodded. "That's fine. We can do one right after school, or even the last period. I can check and see." He glanced at Aunt Vivian. "I have someone else to watch the store tomorrow afternoon, so you don't have to, unless you want to."

"I love doing it. So anytime you need me, go ahead and ask. I don't want regular hours, but I don't mind filling in whenever, especially this time of year, since I know things will slow down after Christmas."

"They always do," he said. January was one of his slowest months. There had been years where he'd considered closing the store completely, if it weren't for the kids getting lessons and the occasional kid coming in to rent an instrument.

They started talking about something else, and Noah enjoyed the delicious soup.

The warm, great-smelling kitchen, good company, and smiles and laughter made him feel like he had come home. No, his siblings weren't here, but it definitely was the kind of place where a person would love to come in and spend some time. But again, maybe that was Grace.

Chapter Twenty

"That Noah Connor is a great man," Aunt Vivian said as Grace put on her coat, wrapped her scarf around her neck, and prepared to leave. She had already worked with Noah that afternoon, the last period in school, with the high school kids. They were scheduled to work with all of the rest of them the next day, which was going to be an extremely busy day, but she had something she had to do first.

"Are you sure you're okay?" Aunt Vivian said.

"I was thinking about what you said about Noah. He really is a good man."

"I just wanted you to know. After all, sometimes we have a tendency to drag our feet, and opportunities that land right in our lap slip out from between our fingers and we don't realize what we've lost until it's gone."

"Are you speaking from experience?" Grace stopped and looked hard at her aunt. It seemed like she was saying more than what the words coming out of her mouth would indicate.

"Well I guess I've never really talked about it, but I was engaged once, and I gave it up for my career. I regretted it the rest of my life.

He went on to marry someone super nice, and he had a great family. Still does actually. And I'm alone. I have you now, which is almost as good as a family, but I always regretted my choice. A career is cold company when you're my age."

"I understand."

"I'm not sure you do. I definitely had financial security, I had accolades from people who appreciated me. My work was good, and I had a lot of people think that I was the best at what I did. But... Looking back over my life, it doesn't compare at all to having children and grandchildren and a family that supports you and loves you. I wish I would've chosen differently."

"Men like Noah don't come along very often." Grace believed that with all her heart. She'd never met another man like him. He was sensitive and kind, but strong and confident as well. And he was a protector, a provider, and most importantly of all of that, he loved Jesus. And he trusted God. He had no fear of the future, and he encouraged her to have a better walk in her Christian life as well. If she were giving someone advice, she would advise them to snatch a man like that up and never let him go.

"Are you sure you're gonna be okay tonight?"

"I'm sure," she said, knowing that it was true. Talking with Noah had given her a confidence that she hadn't had before. Of course, all she was doing this evening was talking with a group of college students as a guest speaker. Thankfully, one of her emails had been an invitation, a late one, since someone else had canceled, and a local college had wanted to see if she could fill in. She was going to play a few notes, probably, but nothing major. Nothing hard, and not for a paying audience. Although she would be paid for her appearance, and hopefully it would be enough to replace Noah's furnace.

With a last wave and goodbye to her aunt, she headed out into the cold. One of the reasons she'd taken this job was because it paid enough, and the other was because it was close by. A private college in the next town. Somehow, they'd gotten wind that she was around, and that played right into her hands.

It wasn't nearly as difficult as what she thought, although she did freeze up for a moment when her fingers touched the keys. Then, she breathed through it and just prayed that whether she messed up or whether she spoke beautifully, that God would use whatever she did for His glory. That took all the pressure off of her, and she could do what she knew she was able to do without thinking about how it might turn out.

It was two hours, and the students were interested and attentive. They were all hoping to be professional musicians, and those were the people she liked to talk to the best. People who were taking a music class just because they had to were no fun to talk to, although sometimes on the rare occasion that she had spoken with them, she tried to think of what she could say that would spark an interest in music for them.

She had no idea whether she'd ever been successful or not, but she had a good feeling about this evening as she said her last goodbyes to the students who now felt like casual friends and got in her car to drive home.

It was late, almost midnight, when she arrived in Mistletoe Meadows, and she parked her car where she usually did, but did not go in the house. She had requested to be paid in cash, and the university had complied with her demands. She had an envelope full of greenbacks, and she wanted to put it where Noah would find it in the morning.

It might be a little bit terrible, but she had noticed the combination that Noah had used when he had unlocked the store, and she thought she could remember it well enough to unlock it herself.

Nerves swirled in her stomach, because she didn't want to get caught. She was hoping she could drop it off without anyone seeing her. She didn't really want Noah to know that she was the one who had provided the money.

She had scribbled "furnace" over the top of the envelope, so he would know exactly what it was for, and she tried to picture how happy and excited he would be to find it.

He would thank God for providing it, and only God and she would know that God had used her to help.

After all, what were the odds that she would have an opportunity to make that much cash that close to where she was, on the exact evening that she needed it? It had to be God.

She was so excited and happy that she had made it to the door and had almost started punching numbers in when she realized there were shadows moving inside.

A light flickered, a face was illuminated, and it was not Noah's.

Her eyes widened.

Was his store being broken into?

She hadn't quite gotten her wits about her to grab her phone and call the police when another face came into the light, looking down at something, the mouth moving, and then as though it sensed her presence, the face looked up, and she looked into Noah's eyes.

His eyes widened, and something like panic entered into them, and then he almost seemed resigned.

He shifted around and came to the door.

She wanted to run, but she couldn't do that. Then she would have to explain why she was there and why she ran on top of it.

She wanted to hide the envelope, but that was the whole point of her visit. So she just stood there, doing nothing, as he opened the door and looked both ways before he said, "Can you come in?"

He didn't ask her what she wanted or why she was there.

She didn't think about that, but just stepped in the store while he shut the door behind her.

"Is everything okay?" he asked immediately, a warm hand coming down on her shoulder. She felt the heat through her coat.

"Everything's fine. What are you doing here rustling around in the dark?" she asked.

Then she realized there were bags on the floor by their feet, which was probably why he hadn't moved her further into the room.

As her eyes adjusted to the light, she could see that there were at least five grocery bags.

"Where were you grocery shopping at?"

He took a deep breath and then blew it out, and then said, "I have a confession to make."

Yeah. She felt her stomach drop and her heart stop. She had thought that he was too good to be true. He seemed like such a great man. But, he was harboring a terrible secret.

"Okay?"

What could the secret be? She couldn't think of anything that she would believe that Noah was doing that was wrong. But it had to be. What else could the explanation be?

"You have to promise me that you won't tell anyone."

"Unless you're doing something illegal."

She was not going to hide information from the cops.

"And I can't lie."

"No. I would never ask you to lie."

That made her heart tremble and start thumping in a regular rhythm again. That was the Noah that she knew. The one who would never ask her to lie. That was the one who she wanted to be with, not this secret hiding person who was doing something underhanded that he didn't want anyone to know.

"I'm the Secret Saint."

He said it so quickly and so softly that she almost missed it, and her mind was racing with so many other things it took a moment to process.

"You're the Secret Saint?" she said, her brows going up.

She swallowed. No wonder the Secret Saint wasn't helping him with his furnace. Or his roof. No wonder. And no wonder he had no money. He was probably spending it all helping other people.

"You are the Secret Saint?"

He nodded slowly. "I'm sorry I kept it from you. There aren't very many people in town who know. I took over from someone who was doing it but had gotten married and was starting a family, and I was the perfect person to pass the torch to because I had no family, and all my siblings were moving out. I was not likely to get caught in the middle of the night doing something and have people ask questions."

"Did I see someone else with you?" she asked, looking around his shoulder.

"You did. I have a helper. He could be considered a second Secret Saint, although he doesn't live in Mistletoe Meadows and... I would really like to not tell you his name."

"All right. You don't have to. I believe you."

That was easy. Because he had always been honest with her, and he had given her the feeling of safety and security enough that she trusted him. Everything made sense, and there were no holes in his story.

"I'm not sure I deserve that, but I appreciate it."

"Of course. And it makes sense to me now why the Secret Saint wasn't helping with your roof or your furnace."

"Right?" he asked, a little grin lifting the corners of his mouth.

"That's right."

She loosened her fingers just a bit, and then, to hide the fact that when she dropped the envelope, it was going to make a sound, she shifted closer and did the only thing she could think of to do. Reached up with her other hand, pulled his head close, and touched her lips to his cheek.

"Good night." She turned around swiftly and walked out the door. She knew he would be looking on the floor because his grocery bags were down there. He would see the envelope. He would almost certainly deduce that it was her, but... He wasn't the only one who had secrets.

Chapter Twenty-One

*N*oah stood staring at the door after Grace walked out. His hand went to his cheek.

She kissed him.

Did that mean what he thought it might mean?

That was crazy.

Why hadn't he stopped her? Why did he just allow her to leave?

He took two steps to the door, then stopped.

Grabbing his phone from his pocket, he texted.

You can't just kiss me and leave.

He hit send quickly, then grinned, looking at the door. He wanted to open it and go running after her, but if she truly needed to leave, he wasn't going to embarrass her with a confrontation.

He wanted to stare at his phone and just wait for her answer to come back in, but he had things to deliver, and... Would she like to help? Now that he'd confessed that he was the Secret Saint, there was no reason why he couldn't ask her if she wanted to.

If she texted back, he was going to invite her.

Grinning, he took a step, and something crackled under his foot.

Had he dropped something out of the bags? He usually worked in the dark, and he had been known to accidentally forget a bag or leave something behind. He tried to be very careful, but mistakes like that happened when he was trying very hard to be secretive.

He bent down, seeing something that glowed white in the dim light on the floor. His fingers wrapped around it just as his phone buzzed in his other hand.

He didn't pay too much attention to the envelope, although it felt like a money envelope, as he glanced at his phone.

> I'm sorry. Maybe you didn't want me to.

He stared at the text. What did she mean? That he didn't want her to leave? Or she didn't want to kiss him?

> Oh, I definitely wanted you to kiss me. Although you missed.

He grinned as he sent that back. Although there was a tight swirl in his stomach, because maybe he'd misread everything.

He fingered the envelope in his hand, barely noticing it as he stared at his phone.

He had told himself he was going to invite her to go with him if she texted him back, and she had. So, even though he could see that she was typing by the three little dots that were bouncing up and down, he sent another quick text.

> Would you like to come deliver these with me?

He closed his eyes as he sent the text.

Please let her say yes. Please let her say yes.

His phone buzzed, and he opened one eye, glancing at it.

It was one word.

Yes.

He couldn't help it. He thought his face might crack from the huge smile that spread across it.

Come on back. I'll load up my truck.

I'm here.

He looked up, and there she was standing on the other side of the door.

He shoved the envelope in his back pocket, shoved his phone in the other, and hurried the two steps to the door, opening it up and letting her in.

"You came back."

What a lame thing to say. But he couldn't think of anything more intelligent.

"Yes. You asked me to."

"You kissed me."

She smiled and looked a little embarrassed.

"You didn't ask me to do that."

"It didn't occur to me to ask. Would you have said yes if I had?"

"I don't know. It seemed like a good thing to do at the time."

He laughed a bit, and honestly, it was all he could do not to step forward, wrap his arms around her, and kiss her properly, the way he all of a sudden longed to. That peck on the cheek was not nearly enough.

But, he didn't want to push her too hard and too fast. She had kissed him on the cheek and had rocked his world, but that didn't mean that she was ready for as much as he was immediately.

"I can help you carry things out."

"Just the bags on the floor."

She nodded, and they gathered up the bags, each of them taking several, and they were able to make it out to the truck in one trip.

They set the bags in the back, and then he went over to her side and opened the door for her.

"Thank you," she said, glancing at him with a shy look as she went by him to get in.

"My pleasure," he said. Meaning every word.

As he walked around, he remembered the envelope in his pocket and pulled it out.

As he got in the truck, he used the dome light to look at it before he slammed his door shut.

"I found this on the floor."

He twisted it around and saw there was writing on the outside.

"Do you mind if I turn the light on again?"

"No, go right ahead," she said, seeming to be interested, but not overly curious.

He flicked the switch, and the dome light shone dimly above them. "Furnace." He read aloud. He glanced at Grace, whose eyes were on the envelope he held in his hand.

"Furnace?" he said as he opened it up and pulled out a huge wad of cash.

"Maybe the Secret Saint found you after all," Grace said, and then her eyes got wide. "Except you are the Secret Saint."

"Yeah." He counted the money quickly and then said, "It's almost exactly enough to cover it. But I know there wasn't anything on the floor earlier. I was back and forth across it a good bit, and the only person to come in was... You." He glanced up at her, and then his eyes narrowed. "Did you rob a bank tonight?"

She snorted, and he had to grin.

"No. I promise you, I did not rob a bank."

He felt the wheels in his mind turn slowly, but they were turning. "But you brought this, didn't you?"

"Yes?" she said, and she seemed concerned. Maybe she thought he was going to be angry.

Was he?

"Why didn't you hand it to me?" he asked. And then he realized what must've happened. She had dropped it when she had kissed him.

"Wait. Never mind about that. Did you only kiss me to distract me so I wouldn't notice that you brought money and dropped it on the floor?"

Oh boy. That made his chest feel empty and hot. He had thought she liked him. He had thought she felt the same way about him that he felt about her. But... She hadn't kissed his lips, she hadn't wanted to touch them. She had only been using the kiss as a decoy. He knew he should be happy about the money, but he had gone from excited that she might like him to devastated that she had only been kissing him so he wouldn't notice what she was doing on the side.

It had definitely worked.

"Noah?" she asked softly, her concerned eyes looking into his.

"You don't really like me like that, do you?" he asked, and he wished the words wouldn't have come out of his mouth. He already knew she didn't, and he had already embarrassed himself enough.

"I don't know," she said. "Yes?"

But she didn't sound sure. It sounded more like a question than a statement.

"So did you or didn't you kiss me to distract me so I wouldn't notice that you dropped money on the floor to pay for my furnace?"

Then he closed his eyes. Why wasn't he just being grateful? Why wasn't he on his knees thanking her? Why was he giving her a hard time because she didn't have the feelings he thought she should?

"I guess it was a distraction. I didn't plan it. But I wanted to. Kiss you, I mean. If that means anything. I wouldn't mind doing it again sometime. Only, I kind of would like it if you kissed me back."

He stared at her. That wasn't what he was expecting her to say. He'd already condemned her in his mind, and it took a little while for her words to pierce through, so he actually heard and understood.

"Really?" he said.

She nodded.

All right, one side of his mouth kicked up, and everything that had been wrong felt like it all settled back down and was just right.

"Okay, maybe we could do that at some point," he said.

"I'm sorry. I shouldn't have just kissed you and run away. And you're right. I did do it a little bit to distract you, but only because I wanted to—kiss you, that is. I just—I guess everything is a little bit crazy for me right now and I don't know exactly how I feel. And—"

"It's okay. I thought you were doing it to deceive me, and I guess I was going to get angry about that. But not necessarily—probably I was just as upset that I thought you liked me the way I liked you, and I was bitterly disappointed to find out you didn't."

"I do. I like you a lot. I've never met anyone like you. Someone that I admire and look up to and... I feel safe and comfortable with you. Does that make sense?"

"I don't know if it makes sense, but I feel more confident when you're with me. I like having you beside me, because I know that you're going to do everything that you can to help and support me. Which was why the idea that you'd kiss me to deceive me was so hard."

His heart had finally settled down a little, and he felt like he could breathe again.

She seemed to understand what he was saying, and she looked contrite.

"I wouldn't have wanted to make you think that. I'm sorry. It just seemed like a really good idea, and I think I was looking for an excuse to kiss you anyway."

"You don't need an excuse," he said, grinning. Boy, she definitely did not need an excuse.

They smiled at each other for a moment before he turned back and started the truck. "If I don't want to have you out all night, we better get started on this."

"I wanted to thank you for asking me to go. I really enjoy helping people. Teaching the kids was so much fun, and it just really gives you a good feeling inside to feel like you're making a difference for someone."

"I know. I agree with you completely. I think sometimes as humans we have trouble letting go of our dreams, the things we think we want. But when God can gently pry our fingers up and shake out of our grasp the things we cling to so tightly, and give us other things to do, things that actually matter in eternity, we are so much more happy and satisfied."

"Well, you're definitely right about Him needing to pry my fingers up, because I wouldn't have let go of my career if it hadn't been for Him."

"Do you think you'll go back?" he asked, feeling kind of casual. But then he realized that it was a question that held a lot of meaning and the potential to affect him greatly.

"I don't know. I guess I've always planned on going back and hadn't considered not. But... I could stay in a town like this."

"Could you live at the poverty level with a music shop owner who doesn't even have enough money to fix his furnace?"

It just occurred to him that his pride should probably be insulted or something, that she was having to pay for an ordinary repair that he should be more than capable of providing for himself.

Of course there was the extenuating circumstance where his sibling had borrowed his emergency fund, but still... If he was the man, he should provide.

"Yes. That doesn't sound the slightest bit off-putting. In fact it sounds exactly like what I would like to do."

"Money makes things easier," he said, and he tried to sound casual, not panicked the way he was kind of feeling. After all, maybe he wasn't ready to have a wife if he couldn't support her.

"It does. I actually have a lot of money put back. Enough that I could live comfortably if I'm careful. I mean, I couldn't live extravagantly, but it would take care of all the basic necessities and a few luxuries, as long as my investments do well. I don't have them in anything too risky."

"Wow." He hadn't even considered that she had money. He thought they were both poor starving artists. He had forgotten that she was successful and well-known.

He supposed he was quiet for a while, thinking, when she said, "Does that bother you?"

He turned into the driveway. "This is where we're dropping the groceries off. I usually park along the street, down the street a little bit, and walk to the house so that I don't wake anyone up. We're a lot closer than I usually am, but I think we'll be okay. We need to be quiet though."

"You don't have to wear a disguise or anything?"

"No. If I see anyone, I'll just tell them that these bags were in my shop and they needed to be delivered. Someone brought them to me. Which is true. My partner dropped them off."

"That's clever. Not lying, but after saying that, they would assume that someone else was the Secret Saint and you were just running errands for him."

"Exactly. I never lie. I don't want to, and I hope I don't start, but yeah. Telling the truth, but leaving the obvious out."

"You didn't answer my question."

No. He hadn't answered her question about whether or not it bothered him that she had money. Because, if he was being honest with himself, it did.

Chapter Twenty-Two

He hadn't answered her.

Grace tried to put that thought behind her. Maybe he was working through some things. And she just needed to give him time. Whatever it was, she couldn't let it bother her. After all, he had been patient with her when she had kissed him and then run out. Even if it was only a peck on the cheek. It was kind of silly for a grown woman to leave that way, and she was a little embarrassed, but she hadn't been quite sure exactly how she felt.

She followed Noah's lead, getting out of the truck and closing the door quietly. They grabbed the bags that were in the back and softly walked through the yard.

An automatic light snapped on, and the sound of a baby fussing reached them.

Noah slowed but didn't stop. He glanced over at her and said, "We might have to use that story I told you."

She nodded, knowing he wasn't saying that they needed to lie, just that they'd found the bags in his shop. Which was absolutely true for her. Maybe she could do all the talking, because she really didn't have anything to do with the bags getting there.

"What's going on?" a voice said from the shadows, and then a woman holding a small baby wrapped in a blanket stepped out into the light.

That was the whimpering they had heard earlier, most likely.

"We have some grocery items for you," Grace began. "And also some blankets and, if I'm not mistaken, a few gifts for under the Christmas tree."

"You are the Secret Saint!" the woman said.

Grace stepped forward. "No. Not at all. I've only been in town for less than a month, so I couldn't be. But these bags were left in Noah's shop and I volunteered to help him deliver them."

"You guys are angels. I couldn't sleep, the baby couldn't sleep, and I didn't want to wake anyone up, so I was out here on the porch pacing. How do you do Christmas when you have no money and your kids are looking at you like you're going to work a miracle?"

"God's someone who works miracles, isn't He?" Grace said, knowing it to be true.

The woman, with tears in her eyes, nodded. "He sure does."

They set the bags on the porch, and then Grace, on impulse, went over and hugged the woman, baby and all.

"If I can do anything for you, just let me know, okay?" she said as she stepped back.

Noah stood behind her; he hadn't said a single word. It was almost like the lady didn't even see him.

"I will. You made my whole holiday season. Thank you."

"Have a good night," Grace said, and then she followed Noah off the porch and back out to the yard and down the walk to the truck. Neither one of them said anything until they were in it and had pulled out on the road.

"Boy, that really makes you feel good," Grace said quietly. "I can see why you would do that. And why you would take all the money you had to buy things for people. We might've been a blessing to her —I think we probably were—but she was more of a blessing to me." She felt better than she had in months. Maybe even years. She felt like she could do anything, because the world was a better place because she'd made a little sacrifice. She hadn't even bought the things. All she had done was deliver them.

"I didn't answer you earlier," Noah said. And her head jerked around. She'd totally forgotten that he'd never said whether it bothered him that she had money and he didn't.

"There is a part of my male pride that says I don't want to be with someone who's got more money than I do. But..." He paused there for a moment, glanced over at her, and then looked back at the road. "That's all it is. Just pride. And so, no. No, it would never bother me. I won't allow it to."

She reached across the seat and touched his arm.

"Thank you for your honesty. It would've rung false if you had just flipped off a no without really thinking about it."

"It maybe bothers me a little that I never had the opportunity to do what you did, and you were so successful at it. I don't want it to, and I'm not jealous. It's not that. It's just... You've really done something with yourself. With your life. You've worked hard and become successful."

"You've been successful. You've successfully raised your siblings. How could you not consider that a success in every way? Here I am, with no family. Nothing. Besides my aunt, whom I haven't visited in years. I think it just depends on your definition of success."

He tilted his head at her, and then smiled and nodded.

"I think you're right. And I think it's God's definition of success that really matters."

"I agree. Trying to become more like Jesus. Knowing God and living your life for the Lord. That's success."

They smiled at each other because they knew what they had been doing that night was exactly right.

Chapter Twenty-Three

*S*unday morning. Noah's favorite day of the week. Well, it used to be anyway, until Sunday afternoons started to get a little long after his siblings moved out. But he still enjoyed the service, and he was really looking forward to going today, because he had texted Grace and asked if Aunt Vivian and she would like to sit with him. She had responded immediately with a yes, and he had to admit, that made his day look a whole lot brighter.

"Good morning," he said as he walked to the gate that led into the Victorian house's yard. Vivian and Grace were just stepping out and closing it behind them.

"Good morning! It's a beautiful day. Very warm for December," Aunt Vivian said cheerfully. He offered his arm to her, and she took it.

Grace finished latching the gate and turned around with a smile. "It really is a beautiful day."

"And I have two beautiful ladies to walk to church with," he said. He offered Grace his other arm, and she slipped her hand in the crook of his elbow.

They started walking down the sidewalk, and Noah had to remind himself to keep his feet on the ground. He felt like he was floating on air. He had been walking to church by himself for a long time, and before that, it was just his siblings beside him for years. And now, he was with a woman he was most definitely falling for. One who loved the Lord and wanted to go to church as much as he did. Who also had a heart to help people the same way he did as well. They had so much in common.

Of course, there were a lot of things they didn't have in common too. He supposed that if he really looked at it objectively, he had as much in common with her as he did with anyone else, it's just... Things he felt were really important were important to her too.

They chatted about the weather and about the community and the festival. They were almost at the church when Roland McBride hurried up to them.

"My mom sent me over here to see if you guys would like to come back to the farmhouse and eat with us. It's just our family, well, Hannah and Ben and Mason, too, but it's a lot, because all of us kids with our spouses and children, but... She put a little extra in the crockpot and she was hoping you would join us."

"My goodness. That's so nice of her." Aunt Vivian looked at Noah and then leaned around him to glance at her niece. "I'd like to take him up on it. I'd love to see Marjorie. We haven't had a good chat for a while."

"We could bring the fajita soup we stuck in the crockpot before church with us. That might help out a little on the food side."

"I'm in if the ladies would like. I told them I would eat with them, so I guess wherever they go, I go too," Noah said simply. He really didn't care where he ate, as long as Grace was there. He enjoyed Aunt Vivian's company too, but she definitely didn't have the draw on him that Grace did.

"All right. That'll thrill Mom. She loves to have company, and she loves the big family dinners too." He grinned and hurried off, joining his wife as she stood in the parking lot talking to Mrs. Tucker.

"That'll be a lot of fun," Aunt Vivian said. "The McBrides are a great family, and there'll be laughter and talking and maybe even some singing after lunch."

"And kids running around everywhere," Noah said. It reminded him a little of his family when they were younger. There were so many of them, it seemed like there were constantly kids flying around. Even after he got older and saw his siblings as immature and too boisterous, it had always been fun.

"This is definitely a change for me. I'm used to things being quiet and slow. And being by myself, or just with another person or two."

"When you get married and have children, you'll have an education, that's for sure," Aunt Vivian said, like it was a given that Grace was going to get married and have children.

Noah couldn't help it. He looked down at her, and she glanced up at him, her cheeks pink.

They didn't say anything, but their eyes met, and something passed between them.

Maybe she saw that he was thinking that he wouldn't mind being a part of that family and children. And maybe—he hoped—she was thinking along the same lines.

Regardless, he seated the ladies, and then went up to the piano. The service flew by, with Pastor Johnson having a wonderful message, although at the end he dropped a bombshell on the entire congregation.

"I've served this community for forty years, and it saddens my heart, but at the end of the year, I'm going to be stepping down. I'm willing to continue until you find a pastor to replace me, but my wife and I have discussed this, and I feel that the Lord is saying it's time. Time to let someone younger come in and take over the Lord's work here. I'll be here if you need me, I'm not going anywhere. But I'll help guide in whatever way you want me to as we search for a new pastor."

Noah was not happy to hear Pastor Johnson was resigning, but it made him hopeful that possibly his friend Mark would be considered as a candidate for taking over. Mark probably wouldn't do it unless he thought it was God's will, though.

The Lord would work things out. Noah knew it, but he could also have his little things that he hoped would happen.

Maybe there was an extra bounce as he played the postlude and thought about how awesome it would be to have his best friend in the world at the same church as him.

Pastoring him.

He couldn't think of anyone else more suited for the job. Or who lived what they believed better than Mark.

Regardless, the service ended, and he escorted his ladies back to their house, where they grabbed the crockpot and drove to the McBrides'.

Chapter Twenty-Four

The McBride's house was crazy. Chaos, laughter, children, and more chaos everywhere.

But as Grace watched Marjorie interact with her children, the smiles and laughter of the grandchildren, and the gentle teasing of siblings, she longed for that for herself.

Noah came from a large family. Maybe he wouldn't want a big family like this, although he seemed totally at home, laughing and joking with the men, helping to carry chairs and set up a table for the children beside the adult table. They carried large plates of food, platters of food, and soon with the ladies' help, everything was ready.

For the first time since they'd arrived, the chaos settled down as everyone bowed their heads and Jones said grace. It lasted a little longer than the typical grace that she said, as he thanked the Lord for the food and asked for strength to be more like Jesus. It was a sincere prayer and one that Grace could honestly say amen to after it was over.

She had been seated with Noah on one side of her and Dr. Hannah on the other.

She hadn't spoken too much to Dr. Hannah, but she knew who she was. And after they passed the mashed potatoes, she said, "So you're one of the McBride children?"

Dr. Hannah laughed. "No. Marjorie just loves inviting people over. And somehow Ben and I have become like children to her, I think. Anyway, she's like a mother to me. She's been a blessing. I work with her daughter, whom you probably have not met, since Dr. Terry just had a baby. She's on maternity leave and will be until the middle of January."

"Oh. That explains things. I wondered why you didn't really look like everyone else."

Hannah laughed. "This family has been such a blessing to me. I used to work in the city, and I didn't really think that family was that important. I was more interested in my career and focusing on that. But I had a few things happen, and I lost my job. And thankfully, Terry hired me, and the McBride family took me in, and I fell in love with Ben, and I don't ever want to leave Mistletoe Meadows." She handed the gravy to Grace and then said, "It's crazy how God works. Sometimes I've resisted, but in the end, I see how His way was best all along. I don't know why I'm still so stubborn. I'm supposed to be a fairly smart person. But sometimes I'm kind of dumb."

Grace laughed and said something in response, but in her heart, she was thinking that God really did work things out. He certainly had shifted things around for her. Hannah looked so happy, like she didn't miss her big prestigious job but was indeed glad to have a slower and fuller life here.

They stayed for several hours after the meal was over, just talking and laughing, and while there was no singing, they did play games and sat outside on the porch, enjoying the sunshine in the afternoon. Finally, she suggested that they go, knowing that Aunt Vivian typically took a nap in the afternoon and was probably exhausted. Sure enough, when they got home, Aunt Vivian excused herself almost immediately to go lie down, leaving her and Noah standing on the front porch.

"Would you like to take a walk?" he asked, as though he too were loath to leave her.

"I would love to."

They stepped off the porch, and their hands brushed once, and then she felt his fingers slide around hers.

It surprised her, but it also felt perfect, and she allowed it, clasping his hand and weaving their fingers together.

She glanced up at him, and he was looking down at her, a serious look on his face.

"Is that okay?" he asked, lifting his brows.

"It's perfect," she said.

They walked slowly along, going in the general direction of his music shop, when she remembered something that she'd seen one of the first nights she had seen Noah.

"Do you write music?"

He huffed out a surprised breath.

"Oh. That's right. You saw me that night."

"That was beautiful music. That melody has been stuck in my head ever since, and I'd love to hear it again."

"I'm glad you like it."

"So you wrote it?" she asked, noticing that he hadn't answered her question.

"I did. I compose some. Nothing is published, but... I enjoy it." He shrugged and then sighed. "It's kind of my little secret."

"Would you share it with me?" She felt bold asking for that. After all, he'd just admitted that it wasn't something that he shared with anyone.

"I'd really like to."

They exchanged a long look as they strolled hand in hand down the sidewalk to his shop.

They didn't say anything else as he opened the door and she stepped in. She stood waiting for him to lead the way back to the room with the piano and his violin.

He took his violin out of the case, then tuned it to the piano and laid it on the top.

Reaching under the bench, lifting up the lid of the bench, he reached in and pulled out a notebook full of music paper, some scribbled on, some notes scratched out. But some neatly organized in a three-ring binder.

"This was the piece I was working on the night you interrupted me. It has evolved into something that I've never done before, and that is a duet between a piano and violin."

He didn't say anything more, but it made Grace wonder if he was writing it for them.

"I didn't really mean for it to go that way, but after I met you... Yeah. It just evolved into that, and multiple nights I've stayed up way past midnight with the music dancing in my head. It's practically written itself."

"May I?" she asked, forgetting until that second that she hadn't played the piano since that fateful night.

But this felt different. It felt right, and she had no fear.

"Of course," he said, but he didn't move to put the music down until she had asked. He set it on the piano and opened it up to the first page. She could easily see the violin part on the top and the piano part beneath that.

Reading the music, she saw that it was going to be a fun piece, a little flirty, and then she turned the page and it got a little more serious, a little more passionate.

"Can I play?" she asked.

"You sure can."

"Will you play the violin part?"

He didn't say anything but picked up his violin and tucked it under his chin.

Typically the piano would have a slight introduction, but with this music, the violin started by itself. A little bit of a sad melody, until the piano came in and kind of nudged it. You could almost feel the introduction as they danced around each other a bit, and then the fun interaction started.

She was so focused on Noah's music and hearing the story, seeing it play out in front of her eyes, that she forgot that she hadn't played in a long time, or that she had been scared to try again. The music flowed out of her fingers as naturally as breathing, and Noah's playing held an understanding and brought out a depth to her own playing that she'd never heard before.

Playing with him was different. Better.

There were some unfinished parts, and they skipped over those, playing what was there, until the end.

The final page had tones of the wedding march and a piece that she often heard at nuptials as well.

There was a slight lullaby, only for a few bars, and then the music ended.

"That's it?" she asked, surprised and disappointed when the music just stopped.

"Yeah. That's all I have so far."

"It's my new favorite music. Oh my goodness." She put a hand to her chest and struggled to find words. "It's the most amazing thing I've ever played. I could see everything."

"What did you see?" he asked softly, curious.

"Back here is where they meet. The violin first, then the piano comes in. They introduce each other, and then they flirt back and forth. Then their courtship on this page, and this was the first kiss."

He dropped to a knee and tucked his violin under his arm.

"You did see it. You understood."

She nodded. "Yes. It was as plain as a movie running in front of me." She turned her head, not realizing he had been so close. Their breaths mingled.

"The part that I was writing the night I met you turned into the courtship part... It all came together once I saw you."

"I don't think I've ever been anyone's inspiration before," she said. Then she paused and took a breath. "You need to play this.

This is what we need to play for the music festival. It has to be this."

He didn't seem upset by her insistence. Instead he searched her eyes, as though trying to read anything else other than what her words were saying.

"For you. We'll play it for you."

"For us," she gently corrected him. Somehow, her hand reached out and touched his cheek.

"I told you before I wanted to kiss you again. You probably ought to say something if that isn't what you want."

She just smiled and pulled him closer, closing her eyes. Of course she wanted to kiss him. How could she tell him that she'd wanted to since the first moment they'd met?

Kissing Noah was just as sweet and perfect as she thought it would be, and made even better by the music they had just played together. And the promise of more to come.

Somehow, his arm wrapped around her, and she slipped her hands around his neck, and they kissed for a really long time.

As she pulled away, she realized he was still holding his violin.

"I'm sorry. I suppose I should've allowed you to put that down."

"Maybe I'll do that now," he said, sounding a little breathless. He had his bow in the same hand, and he expertly set the violin gently on the piano and the bow beside it. "That's better. I wanted to have both hands on you."

They smiled at each other, although in the back of her head, Grace was asking how this was going to work. Was she going to stay here in Mistletoe Meadows? Was he going to chase his dreams in the big city? How were they going to do this together?

But she didn't need to worry about that. Maybe he wasn't thinking about anything along those lines, although relationships weren't really something that she did to be casual and uncommitted.

Still, maybe she could just enjoy the moment and not have to have the rest of her life planned out. Although, it was only fair for Noah to know that she didn't typically go around kissing people without thinking that there was some kind of commitment between them.

He had lowered his head, and she had eagerly joined in a second kiss, but as he pulled away, she looked down and gathered her wits about her.

"That was really nice," she said, and then opened her eyes and looked at him. "I don't want to push for anything, not really, but... I don't typically kiss people without thinking that there's a strong commitment there."

"Yeah. I was looking at you at the table today and wondering if we might have a family of our own sometime, the kids running around, laughter, fun, and music. Lots of music together."

Yeah. That was the kind of commitment she was looking for. And she didn't need any more than that. Not right now.

Chapter Twenty-Five

*N*oah wrote another three notes on the score, tilted his head, changed his mind, erased one of the notes, and replaced it with an E flat. Yeah. That was perfect.

He felt like he was glowing. Kissing Grace had been an experience he didn't even have words for. It left his heart happy and his soul soaring.

He hadn't wanted to part from her, but when she had gently suggested that if they were going to do this music together for the festival, he'd better get it finished, he'd walked her home, given her a sweet kiss before he left, and then walked back home alone.

Maybe he wouldn't be alone much longer.

The thought made him smile again, and a bit of a melody popped into his head.

He jotted those notes down and continued to write.

He didn't know how long it was. He had gotten lost in the music and time didn't have meaning for him when he got into the zone like that, but his phone rang, shocking him out of wherever he was and making him grin again. Maybe Grace wanted to talk to him. Maybe she missed him already.

His smile did not dim when he saw that it was not Grace, but Emma, one of his siblings.

"Hey there," he said as he swiped his phone on.

"Goodness. You sound happy."

"Hello to you too," he said, realizing that he probably did sound a lot happier than usual. That's because he was a lot happier than he had been.

"Noah? Is there something you're not telling me?" Emma asked, and the tone of her voice made it sound like she knew something that he didn't.

"Um, I can't think of anything right off."

That wasn't entirely true. If he sat and thought about it, there were some things. First of all, he didn't tell her that he had been kissing a girl this afternoon. That was kind of unusual. Also, his siblings did not know that he was the Secret Saint in Mistletoe Meadows. So there was that too. He had a few other things that he hadn't shared with his siblings, but not on purpose. Just when they called, it was usually about them.

"I told you he wasn't going to tell us anything," Emma said, and that's when he realized she must've had someone else on the line.

"Why don't we just do a Zoom call?" he asked. "Who else is on?"

"I am," Mia said.

"Me too," Jake's voice.

"Is there anyone not on?" Noah asked.

"I don't think Nate is." That was Mia.

"So... What's up guys?" They didn't typically have big family phone calls unless there was something as a family they needed to discuss.

"We heard you were with someone this afternoon." That was from Mia.

"He's not going to admit it," Jake said.

"Sure I'll admit it. Grace Dempsey has been staying with her aunt in town, and she and I have spent some time together. We were together this afternoon."

"I heard you were kissing."

Noah blinked. He could hardly lie about that.

"I kissed her goodbye." That was true.

"No, this was like really kissing," Mia said.

"All right. Am I not allowed to kiss people?"

"You always told us we shouldn't be kissing anyone unless we were planning on getting married, because kissing someone that you weren't planning on marrying was like kissing someone else's spouse, because you weren't planning on making them yours and it was dishonest."

Jake sounded a little accusatory, and he supposed that Jake had a point. "That's absolutely true. I can't believe you were listening to me. I'm kind of surprised."

"You're changing the subject, Noah," Emma said.

"I was kissing her, and yes, I have plans to talk to her about our relationship, a serious relationship that ends in marriage. But... It's been kind of complicated."

"I don't think you would've accepted that excuse from us," Mia said. "In fact, I think if I were to say that to you, even now, you would give me The Lecture."

"The Lecture?" he said. He didn't realize he lectured. He didn't think he did.

"Yeah. The lecture about how you don't kiss people unless you're serious about them. You know, the one we heard a million times growing up?"

"Listen. I just gave you the lecture that Mom and Dad gave me. Just because you were too young to remember it when they gave it to you doesn't mean that it didn't come from them."

"I remember their lecture, and yours was different."

"How so?" he said. He thought he did a pretty good job of repeating his parents' lectures. After all, he'd heard them the entire time he had been a teenager up until their death.

"You started talking about tongues and lips and hands and body parts, and I don't remember the parents ever needing to say anything like that."

"That's because they were talking to me most of the time when they were giving that lecture, and I didn't need those extra details, because I didn't kiss anybody when I was in high school. Unlike you, who got caught behind the school auditorium when you were twelve with Mindy Lauper. Need I say more?"

Jake was quiet after that. From what Noah remembered, they were playing a game of truth or dare. After that incident, truth or dare was on his list of things his siblings were never allowed to do.

Actually, after that, he'd made sure to have more parties and get-togethers at his house where he could keep an eye on things, and no one was slipping out and doing things they'd regret as adults.

He always made sure the kids had fun, but he made sure they had fun in a way that didn't involve tongues and lips and other body parts that, yes, he might have named to his brother at the time.

"Noah. We're not really giving you a hard time. We just think you need to talk to us about these things." Emma's voice sounded conciliatory.

"I'm sorry. Today was the first day I kissed her, and you're right, I need to make sure that she understands what my intentions are. Because they are exactly what they should be, which is I intend to marry her." He paused. "But I've known her for around seven days. I think it might be a little bit early for me to be proposing."

"If it's too early for that then it's too early for you to be kissing," Jake said.

"All right. I can hear myself in that too."

Was this what having kids was like? They threw up in your face everything that you'd ever said? Weren't you allowed to slip a little?

Truly, he appreciated his siblings holding him to a high standard. And he hoped—maybe it would be a while yet—that they would appreciate the fact that he'd tried to hold them to a high standard as well. Looking back over his life, he didn't regret any of the times where he'd stayed pure and tried to live for Jesus, but he regretted every single time he'd fallen into sin. Not just because the consequences were not good, but because he knew his sin saddened Jesus, and that wasn't what he wanted to do with his life. He wanted to live a life that would make the Lord say, "Well done, good and faithful servant." Not one where certain parts had to be blacked out because they were wrong and bad.

"Guys, I think maybe he needs a lecture about not only are you kissing someone else's spouse, but kissing leads to other things, and those are things that you are directly forbidden to do according to the Bible before you are married. Remember that one?" Mia said, and the others murmured in agreement.

"No doubt he needs that one too. Does someone else want to start it, or do you want me to?" Jake seemed way too eager to lecture him.

"Guys. I promise you, I don't need that lecture. I know exactly what kissing leads to, and... You guys are right."

"I don't want to hear about any shotgun weddings."

"People don't get married just because they get pregnant anymore," Mia said, and he could hear the eye roll in her voice.

"No child should have to be raised without a mother and a father in a loving home." Emma sounded like she was reading off of a pamphlet. Which she probably was reciting from memory, verbatim, things that he had told her.

After all, sin didn't just affect the sinner. It affected everyone around them, and most often it was children who suffered the most.

"And sin doesn't affect just the sinner. It affects the people around them, and most often it's the children who suffer the most."

He laughed. Yup. His words thrown back into his face.

"What's so funny?" Emma asked, as though she hadn't just recited, word for word, what he had been thinking.

"I guess I was just thinking that I get to do this twice if I have children. First, I get to hear it from you guys, and then after I raise my children, they're probably going to do the exact same thing."

"You're gonna be dating again after your children are raised?"

Jake sounded appalled. "Okay guys, we need to dust off the lecture about marriage is forever, and you don't get married thinking that you have an automatic escape hatch with divorce. In fact, divorce should not be a part of your vocabulary. Remember that one, guys?"

"Yeah. I think we got that one on a weekly basis there for a while."

"Guys. Stop. I get it. You want me to hold myself to the same standards that I tried to hold you guys to when I was raising you. Got it."

"We just don't think that that's happening, because from the information that I heard, there was some pretty wild kissing going on."

"I hope whoever saw it said that they could see my hands at all times, and—"

"They did say that, but they couldn't see your tongue."

Noah could feel his face heating. This was not a conversation he ever thought he would have to have with his siblings. He drummed his fingers on the piano. How could he end this phone call?

He thought of something and considered whether or not he was going to say it. All he had to do was say that the furnace wasn't working, and all his siblings would immediately start asking him if he was okay, if he was warm enough, if he needed money... Maybe they would ask that.

No. He wasn't going to burden them with that. He supposed he could let them lecture him as long as they wanted to. And he could know the entire time that they were right. He would've been appalled if one of his siblings had been kissing someone the way he was kissing Grace after only knowing them for seven days. That wasn't very much time at all. Except... He felt like he'd known her forever, and he was confident in knowing that she was the one he wanted to spend the rest of his life with. He just didn't know if she felt the same.

Then why don't you ask her?

He supposed he could have a discussion like that with her. And he'd have to. Because otherwise, she might not understand when he told her that he couldn't be kissing her anymore. Not if he wanted to have any peace and quiet in the evenings in order to finish his composition and not be harassed by his siblings.

Yeah. He and Grace were definitely going to need to have a talk.

Chapter Twenty-Six

"*I*'m heading out to practice," Grace called to Aunt Vivian, who was still in the kitchen, as she put her coat on and wrapped her scarf around her neck.

"All right. Mrs. Tucker is bringing supper, so don't worry about it. And, if you'd like, go ahead and invite Noah and see if he wants to come too."

"I'll do that. I'm pretty sure he'll say yes. When he's been teaching all afternoon, he usually doesn't have time to make supper."

Grace smiled to herself. Whether he had supper prepared for himself or not, if she asked him, she was pretty sure he would say yes. Both of them jumped at any excuse to be able to see the other.

She was still smiling as she walked to the door and picked the mail up from where it had dropped in the slot. It was just one letter, and she was getting ready to set it on the small desk where her aunt kept the mail, when she saw that it was addressed to her.

She turned it over and looked at it a little closer and saw that it was from a prestigious music academy in the city. One she recognized. And one that she had tried to get a teaching position at, but had never been called back.

Maybe this was their formal rejection letter, and she felt like she was in the frame of mind where she could handle it. She wasn't sure what she was going to do after Christmas, but she did have confidence that God had been guiding her steps all along.

Where she and Noah fit into all of that, she wasn't sure.

Expecting a rejection, it took a little while—she was halfway through the letter before she realized that they were offering her a position. It was a faculty position, full benefits, prestigious students... Everything she'd wanted before the incident.

The deadline to accept was December 23rd, the same day as the concert in Mistletoe Meadows.

She looked again at the salary. Wow.

That was more than she'd ever hoped to make, and plenty to live on.

But she thought again of Aunt Vivian, and how she had said that she had made good money, had a great career, but wished she would've made different choices.

But that was Aunt Vivian. That wasn't her.

But... Would Noah be happy moving to the city?

She pursed her lips, stuffed the letter back in the envelope, and set it on the desk right side up so that Aunt Vivian would clearly see her name on the outside.

She would answer it later. Although, she wasn't sure what she was going to say.

Practice went well. The kids were enthusiastic, and even the high school kids seemed like they really enjoyed what they were doing. She supposed in order for them to come and put the time in, they had to really want to. Or else their parents were making them.

Regardless, she didn't care. She was just happy that she and Noah worked so well together, one picking up where the other left off, and both of them seeming to have different strengths and covering each other's weaknesses.

She loved working with him and enjoyed the happy smiles of the children.

The music wasn't bad either, and she was impressed at how the kids had been practicing and how good everything sounded.

"I'm exhausted, but wow, what great practices," she said as the last student left for the evening.

"Same. My goodness, that's a lot of work, but I'm still looking forward to this concert. I've seen the marketing committee's work, and they have drawn up some really great flyers and have some wonderful ads on social media. We just might end up with a big crowd after all."

"Oh I hope so. Thirty years is a big deal, and you should definitely be celebrating that."

"I agree. The town deserves it."

"And you're the perfect person to head it up. You definitely take your responsibilities seriously."

"Speaking of responsibilities, I have the composition finished. I thought maybe we could go over it tonight?"

"Yes, absolutely!" She paused for a moment and then said, "Oh. I forgot to ask. Aunt Vivian said that Mrs. Tucker was going to provide supper for us tonight. She didn't say why. I didn't really ask. Maybe she's going to eat with us. I don't know. But anyway, you're invited."

"That's awesome. I would've invited you to eat with me, but I have nothing ready, and I have no idea what I was going to cook."

"Well don't worry about it any longer. You can eat with me. Even though I'm not cooking."

They grinned together, took one last look around the room to make sure that it was as spic and span as they could make it, and then turned the lights off and walked out the door.

As was their custom, they held hands on the way home, chatting about this and that and nothing important.

On her mind the whole time, though, was the letter that sat on the desk. She wanted to tell him about it, but she just didn't have a good opening. She didn't know whether she wanted his advice or just wanted to know what he thought. She didn't really know where their relationship was going. And while she hoped that he had meant what she thought he meant when he said what he did at the McBride's house about them having children and a family of their own someday, she didn't know how serious he was. Maybe he meant someday way off in the future, twenty years from now. Of course, both of them would be too old for a family and kids at that point.

Gracious, she tried not to let the slight cloud of that thought infringe upon their happy chatter as they made it to the Victorian house on the corner.

He had opened the gate and she'd walked in, when the door opened and Aunt Vivian came out on the porch.

"You look like you're dressed to go out," Grace said, and she tried not to sound disappointed. She was starving and it was already later than what they usually ate. She had been hoping that they would eat as soon as they got there.

"Oh. I forgot that I had a ladies' meeting tonight. You two go ahead and enjoy the delicious meal that Mrs. Tucker made. It's all sitting on the table ready for you. All you have to do is take your coats off and sit down." Aunt Vivian started down the steps, and she patted their arms as she went by. "You two enjoy. Behave yourselves too," she said, giving them a look.

Grace laughed, but Noah seemed to take her words very seriously.

She wondered what was up with that.

Regardless, they stepped up on the porch, and Noah opened the door for her. She walked in, saw the letter on the desk, and remembered once more that she wanted to talk to him about it.

"I think we're on our own tonight," Noah said.

"I think that's what she meant."

"That's probably a good thing. I... I have something I need to talk to you about."

"All right. That sounds serious," she said, not liking the way his tone was more somber than normal. Usually, he teased her, or flirted with her, or they laughed and joked together. Even when they talked about the music festival and the business side of things, his tone was still gentle and kind. But there was a note in it now, a serious note that almost sounded ominous.

It gave her a shiver, but she tried to hide it.

"Do you want to talk before we eat?" she asked, and tried to pretend her stomach wasn't growling.

She didn't fool Noah, and he laughed.

"I think we better eat and talk, because it sounds to me like someone is starving."

"Oh my goodness. I am. Is that terrible?"

"It's been a big day. And we had great practices, but they do take a lot of energy."

They got everything together and sat down to a delicious meal of meatloaf and mashed potatoes.

The aroma of the food drifted up. The house was warm and cozy, and Christmas lights twinkled on the tree and mantle.

They ate at the dining room table, which somehow Aunt Vivian had magically cleared of all traces of her gingerbread houses.

"This is kind of romantic," Noah said, looking around.

Grace had to chuckle just a bit. "I think we've been set up."

"Really?" Noah asked, glancing around again as though clues lay somewhere that he hadn't seen yet. "Do you think the town is setting us up?"

"Yeah, I think so. I mean, Aunt Vivian did not have a ladies' meeting tonight. At least, it came up really suddenly, since I left earlier this afternoon."

"Yeah, that does seem a little suspect. And why wouldn't she eat before she left?" He sighed. "I guess I should just say that I got a phone call from my siblings today."

"Is this what you wanted to talk to me about?" she asked, wondering whether she needed to brace herself or not.

"Kind of. I guess... What I really wanted to talk to you about was my intentions and ask you about yours, but the phone call was basically my siblings reminding me that I had brought them up to not kiss before they were married, unless they were sure that they were getting married, because if you kiss someone that you're not planning on marrying, then you're basically kissing someone you know is going to be someone else's spouse, and isn't it just better to not do that?"

"I can't argue with that logic. Was that your rule?"

He nodded. "And my parents' before that as they were raising me. That, and also kissing leads to other things that the Bible says you're not supposed to do before you're married, so it's just a very good idea to not engage in that type of activity unless you have solid plans towards marriage. And even then to proceed with caution, because until you're actually married, a lot can happen."

"I see," she said. She wasn't exactly sure where this was going, and she was a little afraid that he was going to tell her that he wasn't ready to get married. Or didn't want to.

She tried not to hold her breath.

"So I guess that is why I felt like I needed to declare my intentions and ask you what yours are."

"All right. You first or me first?" She thought briefly about the letter on the desk. Maybe she should tell him about that. It might change things. But... It didn't really change anything for her. The more she thought about it, the more she knew exactly what she was going to do. No matter what Noah did or wanted.

"I guess I wouldn't have kissed you if I hadn't thought that you were the one. I don't go around just kissing anyone. I don't necessarily agree with the way modern society just acts like that's an expected part of any relationship, no matter how brief. I consider kissing an intimate thing that I only want to do with one person, and that's the woman who is, or is going to be, my wife. So I wouldn't have kissed you if I didn't have strong enough feelings for you to think that we could possibly get married." He gave a little bit of a self-deprecating smile. "I suppose I was afraid that I would scare you off if I told you that I wanted to marry you before I'd even kissed you.

But that's on me. I let fear keep me silent, instead of having this discussion a while ago."

"All right," she said, a little uncertain. "So... You're saying you eventually want to get married?"

"To you. And 'eventually' sounds like sometime way far down the road. I suppose... I would get married this evening if we could. I'm not sure." He blew out a breath. "I've prayed about it a lot. I've been asking God to bring the right woman in, and you've felt right since the moment we met. But again, I didn't want to scare you."

"I was in a precarious mental situation when you first met me, so I appreciate your consideration. I also agree with you about kissing. It isn't something that I would do casually with just anyone. I'm not interested in casual dating or relationships. I never have been. I guess being an only child, I always thought I was a little bit too serious, and my friends teased me about it, but that's just the way I felt."

"So we agree?" he asked, and there was a note of hope in his voice.

"Yes. I'm the same as you. I wasn't thinking that we would get married tonight, but I was definitely thinking that we were serious about each other. I'm serious about you. And when you said that we would have children together someday, I assumed that that's what you meant too. That you were serious."

"All right. That's all I needed to hear. Actually, I feel like jumping up and running around the table a few times."

She laughed, but she thought he might've been serious about that, too.

"I actually do have something I wanted to share with you, but... I just got it today, and I didn't want you to think I was keeping anything from you."

"All right?" he said, his brows coming down, like he couldn't imagine what in the world.

"I got a job offer from a very prestigious music academy in the city. It's a really good job offer, great pay, benefits, a prestigious teaching position, my students would be the very best of the best, but I'm going to turn it down. Unless—" she paused for a moment. "Unless you wanted to move to the city and pursue your dreams of becoming a professional musician. If that's the case, I will take this job, and you'll be set. You can pursue your dreams and not worry about having to make money while you are doing it."

His brows went up, and then at the last, they came back down.

"Wow. That's very generous of you."

"When we're married, my money is your money, and vice versa, I assume?"

"I suppose we hadn't talked about money, other than the fact that I don't have any. But yes. That would be the way I would want to do it too. Although while we're talking about things, I suppose I ought to put one more card on the table."

"You're holding cards?" she asked, surprised.

"Just one."

"Right," she said, waiting.

"I had an investor—a representative of Moondoe's Coffee—visit me. Oh goodness, weeks ago. And he made me an offer. It's a good offer. He wants to buy the building that my store is in, then he's going to demolish it and put in a Moondoe's Coffee shop. It's a chain coffee store, no character, and—" he laughed a bit. "All right. So I have a bias against it. Sorry."

"I was reading that. But go ahead. I can divorce your bias from your information and make my own determinations."

He grinned at her, and they shared a laugh.

"That's it. I pretty much was going to dismiss it out of hand. Although our conversation about you having money and me not made me think about it. Is that really that important to me? Am I embarrassed to be married to someone who makes more money than I do? After all, I could sell the business, and I might not have more money than you—not that it's a competition—but I at least wouldn't be in poverty anymore."

"What about your parents? What about your siblings?"

"I know my parents would tell me to sell the business if I wasn't making money at it anymore. Or if I wanted to. I know they wouldn't want it to be a ball and chain around my neck. I'm just not sure about my siblings... I don't know. I was kind of surprised when they all called me and gave me a hard time. I kind of thought they had forgotten they even had an older brother."

"I'm sure they didn't forget. And I'm sure the older they get, the more they will appreciate the sacrifices that you made."

She believed that with all her heart.

"I don't know. I guess I don't really care whether they appreciate them or not. I didn't make them so that someone would appreciate it. I did it because it was the right thing to do."

"That's one of the things I admire about you. And that's one of the reasons that I don't hesitate to say that I'm comfortable making our relationship as serious as it needs to be so soon. Because you are a man who keeps your word and who takes your responsibilities seriously and who takes care of people. I couldn't ask for more, other than that you love Jesus, and to me that underlines everything you do."

He smiled, though her words pleased him.

"I don't know if anyone's ever given me a better compliment in my entire life."

"It was sincere, and every word was true."

His hand moved, and it covered hers where it sat on the table. Their fingers twined together, and they squeezed.

"I suppose because your siblings were harassing you, it means that I'm not getting kissed anymore."

"I think 'anymore' is a pretty strong word. I also don't think that I should allow my siblings to dictate my life."

"All right. I agree with both of those statements."

"But I do think that it might be a good idea for us to... Talk about how soon we want to get married. I feel like I'm pressuring you if I say that. Because... It really is kind of soon in our relationship."

"I guess sometimes we feel like our relationship needs to take the direction that everybody else's relationship does. Society thinks if we do this, or if we do that, it's terrible, and we're too young, we're too old, it's too soon, we're engaged too long. Like, let's just do it the way that we know God wants us to do it and not worry about what the rest of the world thinks."

"I agree with that completely." He squeezed her hand. "So what do you think God wants us to do?"

"I told you. I'm comfortable with whatever you want, whatever you feel like God is leading us to. I'm comfortable going along with it."

She didn't want to be the one in charge. She didn't want to be the one calling the shots. She didn't think that was the way God wanted relationships to work, and she figured that it probably wouldn't be a very good way to start out their relationship.

"Christmas?" he suggested with a lifted brow.

"Well, Pastor Johnson might not want to work on Christmas."

"My best friend happens to be a pastor, and I'm pretty sure he'll marry us whenever we want him to. But I don't want you to rush into something. Is that enough time for you to be ready?"

"Plenty of time. Unless you wanted me to organize some kind of fancy extravagant thing."

"I just want you. Although... I guess none of my siblings are coming in. They might not get to go to my wedding."

"Maybe they'll decide that they're able to make it in for Christmas after all," she said with a twinkle in her eye.

He had to laugh at that.

"I guess it's enough to know that we're thinking about it within the next couple of months."

"Yeah. Or sooner. We could get married before Christmas."

"So you're gonna turn the job down?"

"If you're gonna turn your offer down."

"And you're gonna live with a struggling music store owner?"

"Who just so happens to be a Secret Saint to his town, the pianist at his church, and an upstanding and responsible guy with a great sense of humor. Yes."

"That was a real backwards marriage proposal. Maybe you deserve a better one."

"Maybe I just want one from the right person, and that would be you."

Maybe they had talked about not kissing, and she felt like they both meant it, but perhaps a conversation like this, where they were talking about getting married, needed to be punctuated with a kiss. Regardless, he leaned forward, and so did she, and their lips touched, just lightly, and just for a second or two, before they both drew back, both of them grinning, remembering what his siblings had said and what they had said to each other.

"I'm falling in love with you," he said.

His words warmed her the whole way to her spine and back, and it was easy for her to reply. "I love you."

Epilogue

"And now for our finale this evening, the insanely talented and popular pianist, Grace Dempsey, will play an original piece, a duet, written by and performed with, Noah Connor."

Jones Quebedeau stood at the microphone, looking back and clapping as Noah and Grace walked onto the stage together, hand in hand, smiling.

He carried his violin tucked under his arm, his bow dangling from his finger as he supported the neck. Her music was already on the piano, but the last time they'd practiced, she basically had it memorized. He could not fault her work ethic in any way. But that was the way she lived her life. On purpose, with attention to detail. He thought maybe he had helped her loosen up a little bit, although just before they'd come on, she'd looked at him, and there was a little bit of fear in her eyes.

He hadn't said anything. He just leaned down and kissed the corner of her mouth.

It had made her smile, and they had exchanged a grin, the fear gone.

He knew she'd been praying about it, and he had too, and they'd also talked about whether they were a smashing success tonight or whether they crashed and burned, it didn't matter. God was in control. They knew they had practiced as much as they could, and the rest of the program had gone amazingly well. Now, as they faced the spotlights and Grace settled down on the piano bench, and he stood behind his music stand, bringing his violin up and tucking it under his chin, they would find out shortly how the last number of the evening would go.

He glanced at Grace, and she gave him an almost imperceptible nod, and then he began with the music that had become as familiar to him as his own body.

It was a dance every time, the story of Grace and him. Some of it they hadn't lived yet, but he had one more thing he wanted to do this evening to make their story move along just that much further.

But first, they needed to get through this.

Both of them played with passion and emotion, and the crowd seemed mesmerized. When they were finished, the last notes drifting into the night, there was silence for a few beats, before someone started to clap. Then the entire area around the stage erupted in applause, and people stood to their feet.

They had done it. They had performed the piece that he had written for the two of them, which... In his opinion could never be performed by anyone else as well as it was performed by Grace. And he supposed him, together.

He walked to the piano bench, offering her his hand and helping her to stand. They walked around the piano and bowed to the crowd.

Then, as the applause continued, he turned to Grace and got down on one knee.

"I love you. Will you marry me?"

He was confident in her answer, but he wanted her to have a true, beautiful proposal. Not the backhanded one he'd given her several weeks ago at the table when they had decided that both of them were in it for the long haul and neither one of them wanted to dally around.

Grace's eyes, which had been shining, now filled with tears as her smile stretched wide and huge.

"I love you. Yes. Yes, I'll marry you!"

They smiled at each other, laughing a little, and maybe a tear slipped out, as he stood up and wrapped her in his arms, carefully still holding his violin and bow.

"What a magical night. I love playing with you. Thank you for taking the music I wrote and making it beautiful."

"You wrote our story perfectly. I felt every note."

The applause seemed to get longer and louder, but neither one of them noticed. They were lost in each other's eyes, smiling at the success of the festival, which had broken attendance records by three o'clock that afternoon. And even more people had arrived after that.

Tomorrow would be more festival celebrations and a parade, and he had no doubt that the entire thing would be a huge success. Thanks in part to Grace being willing to take a chance, not just on him, but on herself.

What a great beginning to the rest of their lives.

A Gift from Jessie

View this code through your smart phone camera to be taken to a page where you can download a FREE ebook when you sign up to get updates from Jessie Gussman! Find out why people say, "Jessie's is the only newsletter I open and read" and "You make my day brighter. Love, love, love reading your newsletters. I don't know where you find time to write books. You are so busy living life. A true blessing." and "I know from now on that I can't be drinking my morning coffee while reading your newsletter – I laughed so hard I sprayed it out all over the table!"

Claim your free book from Jessie!

Escape to more faith-filled romance series by Jessie Gussman!

The Complete Sweet Water, North Dakota Reading Order:

Series One: Sweet Water Ranch Western Cowboy Romance (11 book series)

Series Two: Coming Home to North Dakota (12 book series)

Series Three: Flyboys of Sweet Briar Ranch in North Dakota (13 book series)

Series Four: Sweet View Ranch Western Cowboy Romance (10 book series)

Spinoffs and More! Additional Series You'll Love:

Jessie's First Series: Sweet Haven Farm (4 book series)

Small-Town Romance: The Baxter Boys (5 book series)

Bad-Boy Sweet Romance: Richmond Rebels Sweet Romance (3 book series)

Sweet Water Spinoff: Cowboy Crossing (9 book series)

Small Town Romantic Comedy: Good Grief, Idaho (5 book series)

True Stories from Jessie's Farm: Stories from Jessie Gussman's Newsletter (3 book series)

Reader-Favorite! Sweet Beach Romance: Blueberry Beach (8 book series)

Blueberry Beach Spinoff: Strawberry Sands (10 book series)

From Strawberry Sands to: Raspberry Ridge (12 book series)

Swoonfully Jolly Holiday Stories:

Holiday Romance: Cowboy Mountain Christmas (6 book series)

Cowboy Mountain Christmas Spinoff: A Heartland Cowboy Christmas (9 book series)

New and Much Loved: Mistletoe Meadows (4 books and counting!)

Laughing Through the Snow: Christmas Tree, PA Sweet Romcoms (6 short reads)

www.ingramcontent.com/pod-product-compliance
Lightning Source LLC
Chambersburg PA
CBHW031050310726
48969CB00007B/2211